000450245

Jackson County
Medford, OR 975

D0397086

OUTREACH

DATE DUE			
APR 3 0 '93	OCT 21 '94	EC 2 6	R 2
JUN 1 5 '9	MAR 2 0 9	JAN 2 6	MAR 0 4 '9
JUL 1 4 '9	1 1 '95	FEB 8	MY 5 '9
UG 2 4 '93	6/20/95	APR 0	JUL 23 9
SEP 2 2 '93	7/21	MAY - 2 '96	UG 2 5 99
OCT 2 6 '9	2 7 '95	JUL 8	OCT 1 9 '0
EC 1 '93		OCT 9	OV 28 2
AN 2 7 '9	SEP 1 3 '95	NOV 7 '9	5/17/0
MAR 1 1 '94	OCT 0 4	EB 0 7 '97	GP
3 1 '94	NOV 1 '9	APR 2 5 '97	
AUG 2 0 '94	NOV 1 6 '95	EP 1 7 '97	
SEP 7 '94	DEC 2 2 '9		

APR 5 '93

Jackson
   County
      Library
         System

HEADQUARTERS:

413 W. Main

Medford, Oregon 97501

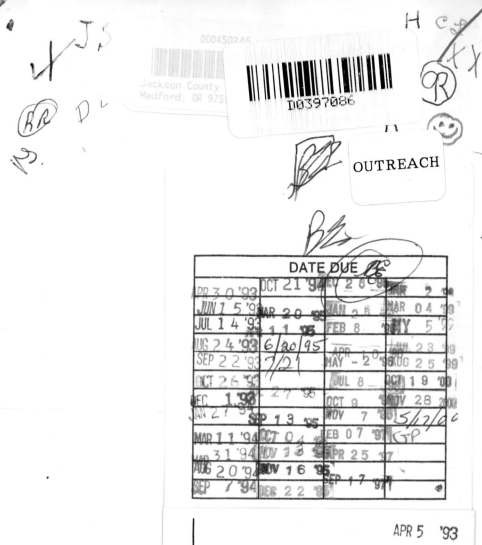

DUREZ CITY BONANZA

Bart Landry had come to Durez City to see an old couple, the Kingstons; on his way he stopped at the Ace Saloon to quench his thirst. That proved to be a mistake. For as a result he happened to be on the spot where he could see and break up a crooked card game. And this in turn led to a fight in an alley with one of the gamblers he had exposed and who was determined to exact vengeance. The mysterious disappearance of the Kingstons immediately after Bart's delayed arrival at their home cast a further cloud over him. And when Bart's gambler foe was found dead, the pall became as black as gunsmoke—or death.

DUREZ CITY BONANZA

Dan Roberts

JACKSON COUNTY LIBRARY SYSTEM
MEDFORD, OREGON 97501

Curley Publishing, Inc.
South Yarmouth, Ma.

Library of Congress Cataloging-in-Publication Data

Roberts, Dan, 1912–
    Durez City bonanza / Dan Roberts.
        p.   cm.
    "Curley large print."
    1. Large type books.   I. Title.
    [PS3568.D2378D87   1992]
    813'.54—dc20
    ISBN 0–7927–1204–8 (hardcover : lg. print)   91–40627
    ISBN 0–7927–1203–X (softcover : lg. print)   CIP

© **Copyright 1965 by Arcadia House**

All rights reserved. No part of this book may be used or reproduced in any manner without written permission except in the case of brief quotations embodied in critical articles and reviews.

Published in Large Print by arrangement with Donald Mac-Campbell, Inc. in the United States and Canada.

Printed in Great Britain

To Neal and Trudy Coleman,
our long time good friends.

DUREZ CITY BONANZA

CHAPTER ONE

Jim Malone's Ace Saloon was the best in Durez City. The tall man packing a .45 with a number of notches on its butt stared into the big mirror over the bar with quiet interest in his pale blue eyes. Because he was so thin he looked even taller than he really was, and his black sateen shirt and Oregon breeches tucked into boot tops showed the dust of a recent long journey.

But the tall man's face gave no hint of weariness. Instead, the lined, bronzed features suggested strength and assurance. No one could have called Bart Landry handsome, but many a young miss along the trail had lost her heart to his manly looks.

Just now the hint of a derisive smile played about his full, good-natured mouth as he stared into the mirror at the reflection of the poker game going on at the table just behind him. He'd been in Durez City only a half-hour, and it seemed he might be on the track of some action right off!

The Ace Saloon was typical of a lot he'd been in, with a long bar along one wall, some tables and chairs with pictures of race horses, burlesque actresses and prize fighters on its walls. It was lit in daytime by a window high in the rear wall and whatever light filtered in through the head-high swinging doors of the entrance. At night, a couple of wagon-wheel chandeliers with lamps set on them at intervals provided a yellow, shadowy illumination. There were also a few single lamps set along the back of the bar.

It was nearly ten o'clock, and the place was filled. The bar was crowded with loud-talking, laughing cowhands and locals taking it easy after a hard day. Bart knew no one in the place, and he figured no one knew him. He liked it that way. But he didn't like what he was seeing happen at the poker table.

Rotund, bald Jim Malone came up to him, quickly lifted his empty glass and asked, 'The same again, mister?'

Bart nodded, his weathered Stetson well back on his head. But his pale blue eyes were fixed on the mirror. From somewhere in a dark corner he heard a woman laugh softly. His right hand instinctively touched the butt of the .45. He found himself tense from waiting. It had to happen pretty soon!

Jim Malone came back with his drink. The fat man eyed him. 'Double whiskey,' he said, and waited for his money.

Bart threw across some coins along with a tip but otherwise paid the saloon owner no attention as he lifted the glass of amber liquid to his mouth and gulped it half down. The fat Jim Malone gave him a suspicious glance as he moved on to serve another customer. It made Bart wonder if he knew what was going on.

Suddenly one of the men at the poker table jumped up and cried in an angry voice, 'This is a crooked game!'

At once a strained silence fell over the noisy, crowded saloon. Men turned to stare at the group around the table.

Bart was not surprised by the accusation. From the time he'd started watching the game in the mirror, he'd been aware of the dealer's manipulations. Now he turned around with the others and with a lazy smile regarded the drama being played out at the circular table.

The man making the accusation was past middle age, had a crop of gray stubble on his face, and a heavy paunch in contrast to a rather skinny body. His clothes were essentially those of a city man, soberly dark, and he wore a rather battered hat of the same black shade. But everything he wore was so dirty and threadbare he looked more like the caricature of a gentleman than a gentleman.

Now he directed a forefinger at the slick-looking dealer of the game and said, 'I saw you slip cards into the pack just now!'

The dealer, a youngish blond man named Clancy Evans, who had been running the games in the Ace since he'd come to Durez City three months before, gave him a knowing smile.

'You've had one too many, Doc,' the blond

3

man suggested in a tolerant voice. He had a certain innocent, boyish charm that illy matched his profession and his methods.

The man with the paunch turned purple with indignation. He said, 'Don't talk to me like that, you crook!'

One of the other men at the table, a big man with a heavy mustache, grinned at the indignant accuser and said, 'We know the stakes have gone beyond you, Doc. It's okay if you want to drop out of the game.'

The dealer nodded, his smile still broad and easy. 'Sure thing, Doc. You just retire and get it out of your system.'

There was a general laughter around the table and all through the saloon. Bart felt this confirmed what he'd already come to believe. The man called Doc was undoubtedly the town drunk. His whole appearance and manner indicated it. And no one seemed ready to listen to his well-founded accusation.

The man with the stubble of gray beard blinked around the hilarious crowd. He licked his purple lips nervously, disbelief on the mottled face that had once had dignity and gentle humor, judging by his drink-ravaged features.

He shook his head as if he could not understand. 'Isn't anyone going to listen to me?' he demanded with a note of despair in his voice.

'Yes, mister, I am.' The reply was drawled out, but in a tone loud enough to be heard throughout the saloon. It was Bart who spoke.

Clancy Evans jumped to his feet, the innocent boyish charm leaving his white face as he glared at Bart. 'You aim to mix in this, mister?' he asked in a soft voice.

Bart nodded slowly, the .45 now out of its holster and directed at the gambler. 'I aim to,' he said.

The other players at the table eyed him with consternation. They were beginning to believe they were being cheated but wished nobody had gone to the bother to inform them.

The man with the big walrus mustache cleared his throat uneasily. 'You mean to say you're accusing Clancy of cheating when you ain't even sittin' in on the game?'

Bart jerked his head toward the mirror behind him. 'I saw enough of what was going on in there. I had a better view than any of you could have had.'

Clancy Evans threw an appealing glance in the direction of proprietor Jim Malone, who was scowling behind the bar. 'Why don't you throw these two cheapskates out, Jim?' he asked plaintively. 'We want to go on with our game.'

Before Jim could answer, another voice spoke up from the shadows, and a huge man emerged to stand beside the one known as Doc. He said,

5

'Before we get to any roughhouse stuff, I'd like to know what these gents are complaining about.' The words were spoken with the weight of authority, and Bart was quick to notice the silver star on the sheriff's gray plaid vest.

'Clancy is running a crooked game. I spotted him slipping cards in the deck just now.' He glanced toward Bart. 'And this gent backs me up.'

The sheriff turned inquiring eyes on Bart. He was an old, square-faced man with heavy jowls and bushy gray eyebrows. His voice was gruff as he asked, 'Is that the way it is, Stranger?'

Bart smiled. 'Sure.'

The sheriff gave Clancy Evans a piercing glance. 'Seems like these two are pretty sure of themselves, Clancy,' he said. 'I reckon you owe the gents at the table an explanation.'

'I've nothing to explain,' Clancy complained. 'I don't know what they're talking about! A drunk and some trouble-maker who just rode into town! You going to take their word against mine?'

There was a low murmur of approval for this spirited speech.

Bart waved his .45. 'If you'll make a little check, Sheriff, I think the matter can be settled.'

The sheriff hesitated and then, drawing his own heavy gun from its holster, said, 'I'll do just that. Meanwhile, I'll ask you to put back that .45 where it belongs. I'll do the gun-totin' around here, if you don't mind!'

Bart shrugged and slipped the gun back in its resting place again but kept his hand near the butt. 'If you'll check the dealer's coat, Sheriff, you should find a metal clip with some cards just inside and under the left arm.'

The sheriff was already on his way, and as Clancy took a step back defensively, the big man shot a hand forward and ripped open his fancy black coat to reveal the metal clip holding cards just as Bart had predicted. The room reacted with a surprised rumble.

The sheriff ripped the clip from the gambler's coat and regarded first it and then Clancy Evans with disgust. 'I ain't seen one of these things since the last hanging in Durez City,' he said. As the murmurs of the onlookers rose, he glared around at them and announced gruffly, 'That don't mean there's likely to be another. I'm the law around here, and I'll deal with Clancy as I see fit.'

Jim Malone had come from behind the bar and now stood beside the gambler. 'There must be some mistake, Sheriff,' he said. 'I know Clancy runs a straight game. I'd say someone framed him by putting that thing in his coat without him knowing it.'

The sheriff looked unimpressed. 'That's a tall story, Jim. I doubt if these folk would want to believe it.'

7

Clancy Evans spoke up unhappily. 'It's the truth! I've never seen that thing before.'

Now one of the others at the table, a spare, solemn-looking man, rose and said, 'I suppose next thing you'll tell us you don't even know what it's for!' There was annoyance in his voice. 'I, for one, want all the money I lost in this game returned!'

'And so do I!' the man with the walrus mustache agreed as he jumped to his feet.

The sheriff turned to Clancy Evans. 'Dump whatever you've got on the table with the rest of that cash, young man,' he ordered. The gambler glanced Jim's way and, seeing no real support from that direction, emptied his pockets and wallet on the table.

The man who'd made the original complaint, the one called Doc, looked across at Bart and grinned. Meanwhile, anger was rising among the occupants of the saloon, many of whom had undoubtedly been at the table with Clancy Evans on former occasions. There were loud expressions of outrage and debates as to what should be done.

The sheriff called loudly for their attention. 'Clancy Evans is going to be dealt with by the law and not Judge Lynch,' he warned them in his gruff voice. 'And anyone who has a different mind can argue it out with my Colt!'

Since no one seemed in a mood to tangle with either the sheriff or his Colt, the big man led

Clancy Evans, abject and with head down, out of the swinging doors of the saloon. Meanwhile the men at the table were dividing up the hefty amount of cash. Jim Malone had gone back to his bartending with an angry expression on his moon face.

Bart Landry swung around to the bar again and finished off his whiskey. A couple of nearby cowpokes congratulated him on his stand, and Doc came over.

'Let me thank you, Friend,' he said, shaking Bart's hand. 'I owe you a lot for backing up my play just now. My name is Webster, Dr. David Webster.'

Bart's pale blue eyes studied the mottled face. 'You practice here in Durez City?' he asked.

'I did at one time,' Dr. Webster said with a slight cough of embarrassment. 'Failing health has obliged me to retire, and the town was forced to call on the services of another medical man. He is young and healthy, if somewhat less than experienced, if I may make that small criticism.'

Bart showed grim amusement. 'So you do no doctoring at all.'

The other man pulled at his coat lapels in a manner that must have been impressive when he'd been a doctor but was somewhat ridiculous now. 'Only in a dire emergency,' he said in a professional tone. 'I have more than once been called upon to probe for a bit of lead in an

9

unfortunate's carcass in one or the other of the town's saloons. But only urgent cases such as these grasp my attention these days.' He stepped up to the bar beside Bart. 'I insist that you join me in a drink.'

Bart did not want to offend the man, but he was anxious to get about his own business. However, it struck him that Dr. David Webster might be of some value in giving him information.

'A double whiskey,' he told the battered man with the paunch.

'A proper male drink,' Dr. Webster said with an approving look on his unshaven face. 'I have an unfortunate proclivity for brandy myself.' He sighed. 'I fear it may have undermined my health.'

Bart gave him a shrewd glance. 'I suppose it depends on how much you drink.'

The doctor frowned. 'I cannot agree with you there, young man. I like to think the damage is caused by the inferiority of the brand. And may I say that in all of Durez City, I have not been able to find a brandy to my taste.'

'You've lived here long?'

'Came with my wife twenty years ago,' the doctor said. 'May she rest in peace. A good woman, but not up to the arduous rigors of the West. One might say she pined away.' He sighed. 'Now I am on my own.' Studying Bart

10

with red-eyed interest: 'You're a newcomer, eh?'

'Yep. Just rode in a half-hour ago.'

'Aim to stay long?'

The thin man shrugged. 'Depends.'

Dr. Webster glanced around furtively and then, leaning close to Bart, said in a hoarse whisper, 'I have to warn you, stranger. You got off to a bad start. You notice we're not gettin' fast service from Jim Malone.'

Bart glanced along the bar and saw that the fat man had his back turned to them. He smiled at the doctor. 'Looks that way.'

The doctor rubbed his stubbled chin. 'They won't forgive what you done in a hurry. I wouldn't stay in Durez City long, mister.'

Bart raised his eyebrows. 'You've been here long enough. You spoke your piece, and you're not liable to leave in a rush, are you?'

Dr. David Webster showed embarrassment again. 'It so happens they don't consider me worth drilling.' He paused. 'I might as well tell you, since you'll find out if you stay here, anyway. I don't rate high in these parts nowadays. I don't imagine one of those men at the table would have listened to me if you hadn't spoken up.' The doctor banged his fist on the bar and shouted: 'Service! Bartender!'

Jim Malone turned to them with insolent slowness and came down to where they leaned against the bar. 'Double whiskey, and a brandy for you, Doc?' he asked.

11

'Bring me a full bottle, Malone,' Dr. David Webster said grandly. 'I have the money.'

When the fat man went off, scowling, to fill their orders, Bart turned to the doctor, who was more than a head shorter than himself.

'You know a Kingston family around here?' he asked.

The doctor smiled at the name. 'The Kingstons! Of course! A fine old couple! They live in a white frame house just a short distance from town.'

'Not far from here, then?'

'Only about a ten-minute ride,' the doctor said. He studied Bart with some surprise. 'You know that old couple?'

'I know of them,' Bart said carefully.

'Sad! Neither of them is very well these days. But they're people of remarkable courage. Somehow they manage on very little. I expect a few of the wealthier people in town help them. And I have offered them medical advice gratis whenever they require it.'

The bartender came back with their drinks and frowned while the doctor carefully paid out their cost plus a small tip. He walked away again as if it had all been a most regrettable experience.

Doc Webster chuckled. 'Jim sure is peeved.' He poured himself a full glass of brandy. 'Your health!' he offered. 'I trust it always continues better than this dubious brew.'

12

After they'd had their drinks, Bart said, 'This is a quiet town?'

'Quiet enough,' the doctor agreed. 'But then Jim Malone and his crowd have everything pretty much their own way. He owns this place and the Round Barrel Saloon on the next street. They are the two largest money-making establishments in the place.'

'Anyway, it seems you have an efficient sheriff.'

Doc Webster drew a soiled linen handkerchief from his pocket and fastidiously wiped his lips with it. Then, after glancing cautiously about him, he leaned toward Bart with a confidential air.

'I hope you didn't let that little scene just now fool you,' he said in a low voice. 'Sheriff Hill is Jim's paid man.'

Bart frowned. 'If he's the owner's friend, why did he go through with exposing that gambler just now? I have a hunch Jim Malone knew his man was cheating.'

'You guess right,' the doctor agreed. 'Jim is not above setting up a crooked game as long as the blame, in a showdown, can be put on someone else. The sheriff saw he had to go through with it once you'd spoken, so he worked it so he could get Evans out of here safe.'

'He won't put him in jail?'

'Clancy Evans! Not likely! He'll let him leave

13

town and say he decided it was the best thing. Then Jim Malone will bring in another crooked card dealer, and the game will go on with nobody hurt.'

Bart said, 'You seem very sure of this.'

'I've seen it happen too often before,' the doctor said, pouring himself another three fingers of brandy and then downing it at a gulp. 'Politics is always a dirty business,' he said. 'But in Durez City we've got a special brand that is downright filthy.'

'Then nothing much was accomplished by you complaining and my backing you?'

'I got a pocketful of cash.' The doctor chuckled, patting his trousers. 'I figure that's worth-while.'

The tall man regarded him with a thin smile. 'I see you are a realist. You have no idea of reforming Durez City.'

'Just as long as I can keep up with my brandies,' the doctor said. 'One can't ask for too much.' He paused. 'You aim to go out to the Kingstons' tonight?'

Bart nodded. 'Yes.'

'They'll be in bed by now.'

'Then I'll have to rouse them.'

Dr. David Webster considered. 'You are welcome to stay the night at my place. It's a trifle disordered at the moment, I fear, but still there is plenty of room.'

Bart shook his head. 'I got business with the

14

Kingstons, pronto.'

The doctor finished his drink. 'Watch your step while you're in town.' He jerked his head toward Jim Malone. 'The fat man has a way of paying off his enemies.'

Bart nodded and started for the swinging doors. As he walked along, he was conscious of interested stares following him, and from the corner of his eye he caught a glimpse of a sneering smile on Jim Malone's fat face as he leaned over the bar to speak to one of his customers. As Bart touched his hand to one of the gray swinging doors, a burst of loud, harsh laughter trailed after him.

He stepped out into the cool, starlit blueness of the street and for a moment stood on the wooden sidewalk. Then he turned and walked down toward where his bay horse was hitched. The street was almost completely deserted, and as he approached the bay it nickered nervously.

Something in the silent and brooding atmosphere of the dark street put Bart on the alert. His tall, lean body stiffened and his thin face went hard as he slowed his pace just a trifle. Only a few steps now separated him from the hitching post where he'd left his bay. His pale blue eyes quickly took in the surroundings. A few feet ahead on his left, there was a narrow alley between two ramshackle buildings.

As he neared the alley, his hand touched the butt of his .45. Then, without warning, a figure burst upon him and he saw the gleam of a knife upraised to strike. He quickly grappled with the attacker and even in the frantic struggle was able to identify the hate-twisted face of the young gambler, Clancy Evans.

Evans had the strength and agility of youth and made a formidable opponent. He also knew how to wield the knife, and twice he ripped through Bart's shirt to make stinging thrusts that seared his flesh. But as they struggled back and forth in silent desperation, Bart knew no serious wound had been inflicted on him yet. The bay whinnied as the two men fell onto the wooden sidewalk and rolled in combat. Bart drove hard fist blows to the body and face of the young man.

The two men panted fiercely as they battled in the near-darkness. Once Evans lost the knife and then clawed savagely until he'd found and regained it. Meanwhile, Bart was inflicting his share of punishment, and the young gambler was showing signs of weakening. Somehow Evans freed himself and ran back a few steps, the knife again in his hand. Bart weaved toward him and, parrying off a lunge from the knife, grasped Evans' wrist in a killing grip that forced the shining steel from his clenched fingers. With a quick follow-up he brought a heavy right to the gambler's jaw that actually sounded with a pulpy crack as Evans staggered back to

16

fall into the street at the sidewalk's edge and lie very still.

Bart lost no time mounting the uneasy bay and heading in the direction the doctor had told him the Kingston home was located. The houses of Durez City thinned out, and he found himself on a narrow road. He pushed on through open country and at last came to a plain white house set a distance from the road that he guessed must be the Kingstons'.

Getting down from the bay, he moved swiftly to the door and pounded hard on it. There was no answer, so he used his fist on the wooden panel again. Then he heard a rustling from above as someone moved about in the bedroom. After a short wait there was the sound of someone on the stairs.

A man's feeble old voice called out from the other side of the door, 'Who's there?'

Bart stood motionless, tall and thin. 'Bart Landry,' he answered.

There was a pause. Then the door opened, and a short, white-haired old man in a nightshirt and trousers hastily slipped on stood peering at Bart, holding a lamp in his hand.

'So you've come!' he said.

Bart's bony face was grave. 'I've come,' he agreed.

CHAPTER TWO

Bart was up early the next morning and made himself breakfast. The small farmhouse was pleasant enough, although sparsely furnished. Most of the rooms had a threadbare appearance and, with the exception of the kitchen, were filled with a stale smell of dead air. The Kingstons had let all their stock go except a cow and a few chickens, kept to provide eggs and milk for their own needs. He'd stabled the bay in the small barn out back and had already begun to settle down.

He'd cleaned the wounds on his side and treated them. Evans hadn't done much damage. He'd finished breakfast and looked after the bay and was taking a walk around the grounds surrounding the house when he heard the sound of hoofbeats. He shaded his eyes from the bright sun and saw that the rider was approaching from up the road rather than from the town. A second glance told him it was a girl!

He walked across the field and down to the road to meet her. She was not riding fast, and it was several minutes before she reined her lovely chestnut mare to a halt and stared down at him in surprise.

'Who are you?' she wanted to know. She was a pretty girl, with long brown hair tied with a ribbon at the back, wearing a fawn hat and a light brown riding habit.

Bart smiled up at her. 'My name is Bart Landry. Now could I ask you the same question?'

Her pert face still showed doubt. She said, 'I'm Eve Driscoll.' And her tone indicated she expected him to recognize who she was by her name.

Bart's eyes held a humorous twinkle as he held the reins for her to dismount. He said, 'Well, Miss Driscoll, what can I do for you?'

The attractive young woman in the riding habit eyed him suspiciously. She said, 'I've come to see the Kingstons. I come almost every day.' She nodded toward her saddle-bags. 'I've brought some things for them.'

All at once Bart remembered the doctor's remarks that the wealthier people in town joined in helping the Kingstons. He smiled at the girl. 'I suppose you do this regularly?'

The pretty face showed annoyance. 'What if I do?'

'Nothing. I think it's very kind of you.'

She ignored his comment, went to the mare, opened a saddle-bag and pulled out a big paper bag which obviously contained food. Then, returning to him, she said, 'I'll go in and see Mrs. Kingston now.'

He barred her way. 'I'm afraid you can't.'

Eve Driscoll looked at him angrily.

19

'Nonsense. Of course I can.'

Bart's expression turned blank. 'I'm sorry, Miss Driscoll,' he said. 'You can't see them.'

'Why not?' she demanded, now beginning to show signs of fear.

He sighed. 'They're not here.'

'Not here?' She gave a gasp. 'What's happened to them?'

The tall man shrugged. 'They've just gone.'

Eve Driscoll's expression was one of disbelief. 'I don't think you're telling me the truth,' she said. 'They must be in there.'

'Look if you like,' Bart said with resignation in his tone.

In answer the pretty girl gave him an angry glance. As he stepped back, she pushed past him into the house. He stood waiting and watching after her with a strange expression on his bony face. After some minutes she returned.

She walked slowly down the path, her bag of food still in her hands, and came to a stop before him. Her voice sounded awed as she told him, 'They have gone.'

'I told you,' he said quietly.

'But where? And why?' she wanted to know.

'They've gone away on a holiday,' he said.

Eve showed signs of returning anger. 'But that's ridiculous,' she said. 'They never go anywhere. They have no money for vacations!' Then, a new idea striking her: 'Who are you and what are you doing here?'

20

'I'm a friend,' he said. 'I'm going to look after the place.'

The girl's round, pretty face held a troubled expression.

'It's early in the morning and they're gone!' she exclaimed. 'It's the most ridiculous thing I've ever heard!'

'Just because you've come here day after day and found them here doesn't mean it always has to be that way,' Bart told her patiently.

'But it doesn't make sense!'

He smiled again. 'A lot of things in life don't.'

Her eyes fixed on him. 'Just what are you to the Kingstons? And why should they leave without telling anyone they were going or where they were planning to go?'

'They left in the middle of the night,' he said. 'The old man figured it would give them a start when it was cool.'

Eve Driscoll listened, but she had doubt written on her pretty face. 'And where are they going?' she asked.

'To their nephew's in the south, in Santa Ana City. It's a couple of days drive.'

'They're much too old and ill to take such a trip,' she said.

He shrugged. 'You can tell them when they come back.'

'That's not funny!' She looked down at the bag of food she was carrying and said, 'What

21

am I supposed to do with all this?'

'Take it back with you.'

'We don't want it or need it!'

He smiled thinly. 'Then leave it here. I am not much of a cook. I could do with a few dainties.'

The brown eyes searched his face. 'You're sure they are all right?'

Bart was impressed by her concern for the two old people. He said, 'I've told you all I can.'

She sighed and touched a hand to her temple. 'It's such a fantastic story I find it hard to believe.'

'I hear truth is stranger than fiction.'

'When will they be back?'

'That's hard to say.'

Her eyes narrowed. 'You must have some idea!'

He shook his head. 'They didn't say a word about coming back.'

Now he could see she was becoming frightened. She looked toward the frame white house, so deserted and bleak now. 'This is their home. They wouldn't just drive away and leave everything behind them without saying when they will return.'

'It does seem odd,' he admitted. 'But that's the way it happened.'

'When did you get here?'

'Late last night.'

'And they didn't even wait until morning to leave?' She was plainly shocked.

'They were in a hurry, I guess.'

The girl shook her head. 'Please, Mr. Landry, I am not a child. I don't believe in fairy stories.'

He raised his eyebrows. 'You would rather I lied?'

'I think you are lying,' she said, her voice sharp.

'I'm sorry.'

She moved a few steps from him as if to test her freedom. When he made no move to stop her, she turned and looked back with a strangely puzzled expression. 'I'll have to tell my father about this,' she said. 'I expect he'll come here to see you. He won't be satisfied, either.'

Bart followed her a step. 'What do you think I've done?'

'I don't know!' There was a tremor in her voice.

He took a step nearer. 'Surely you don't think I've murdered them?'

She moved slightly away from him again. 'You said that; not I,' she pointed out.

Then, with an awkward gesture, she shoved the paper bag into his hands. 'You may as well take this.'

'Thanks.'

'It was meant for them,' she said with a deep

23

sigh. She shrugged. 'Now it doesn't matter.'

He followed her to the mare and stood while she mounted the beautiful chestnut.

'Come back again,' he said, 'any time.'

She leaned forward, grasping the horn of her saddle, her face serious. 'My father will come to see you.'

'I can't tell him anything more than I've told you.'

'He won't be so easy to put off,' Eve Driscoll warned him.

'I suppose not,' Bart agreed.

The brown eyes appealed to him. 'The Kingstons will come back, won't they, Mr. Landry?'

'It wouldn't surprise me,' he said.

'Is that the best hope you can offer?'

'I'm afraid so.'

The girl wheeled her horse around and called back over her shoulder, 'Whatever you've done, you'll pay for it! My father will see to that!' And with this parting threat, she let the chestnut gallop off and left him standing watching her vanish in rising dust.

Bart made his way back to the field where he'd been standing when Eve had ridden by, walked over close to the barn and studied a square area of ground that had been hastily spaded and where the earth had been replaced by lantern light last night. If anyone saw this, he knew they would become instantly

24

suspicious, and so he stood debating what he should do.

Glancing around, he saw a pile of weathered gray lumber by the front of the barn. He decided to remove the top boards from this and scatter them over the freshly dug earth. By the time he'd placed a dozen or so over the telltale spot, he was satisfied with his camouflage. It looked like another carelessly stacked lot of lumber. The loose, dark earth beneath was concealed well enough not to attract notice. It was another problem taken care of. He was glad Eve Driscoll had not found the spot, or her suspicions would have quickly changed to convictions.

Bart had scarcely finished with the lumber when he heard the sound of a horse approaching again. But this time it was from the direction of Durez City. He quickly made his way around to the front of the buildings in time to see a strange figure riding toward him at a reckless pace.

Doc Webster was spurring along a bedraggled-looking gray horse and waving his arms and yelling at the same time. Bart stifled an impulse to laugh, ran out and helped the still shouting rider by holding onto the gray steed's reins until Doc slid from the saddle and limped toward him.

'Haven't had a ride like that in years,' he puffed. 'Last time was when a Mexican came

25

into town and told me his squaw wife had just had quintuplets. Turned out to be only triplets. I hadn't heard him right. But I was needed anyway.' He paused to take out his dirty handkerchief and, removing his hat, mopped his brow.

Bart, still holding onto his horse, asked, 'What's the excitement?'

Doc Webster's purple, bearded face looked alarmed as he stuffed the handkerchief away and shoved his hat on once more.

'Bedlam has broken loose in Durez City,' he exclaimed. 'They found Clancy Evans dead!'

'Dead?' Bart said. 'I didn't do it!'

'They think you did, and that's the same thing,' Doc insisted, glancing nervously at the road from town as if he half expected to see a posse rolling up.

'We had a fight,' Bart admitted. 'He came out of an alley at me with a knife. I didn't want to use a gun, so I grappled with him. It was some tussle, but in the end I knocked him out and he rolled over into the roadway.'

'Hit the back of his head on a boulder and smashed it like an eggshell,' Doc Webster said. 'I was there when they found him a couple of hours ago. The sheriff is out looking for you.'

'I didn't kill him!' Bart protested. 'It was an accident.'

'You try and prove that to Sheriff Hill,' Doc Webster said with a despairing air. 'Don't think

26

he and Jim Malone are going to miss a chance to get you in serious trouble after last night.'

'At least they won't know where to find me,' Bart said.

The man with the gray stubble of beard looked miserable. 'I'm afraid they do, Son. I guess maybe I had a mite too much brandy last night, and I was talking with some of the boys at the bar and told them you were a friend of the Kingstons. Jim Malone heard me. The posse is headed this way now. That's why I came to warn you.'

Bart frowned. 'I can't leave here yet.'

'You better if you want to breathe awhile longer!'

'There must be some way to prove I didn't kill Clancy Evans,' Bart said; 'someone who will listen to my side of the story.'

Doc Webster nodded. 'There is. But he can't help you right now. If you could swing around into town and get to Mayor Peters, he'd see you were treated fairly. He's the town undertaker, and the only one not under the thumb of Jim Malone.'

'No time for that now,' Bart said with a sigh. 'Swing into the saddle again and follow me.'

Doc Webster's mottled face was bewildered, but he gave no argument and clambered back onto the gray. Bart ran toward the barn, went inside and got his bay. Quickly he threw the saddle on it and strapped it down; then he led

27

the horse to Doc and gave him the reins.

'Get out of here as quickly as you can,' he instructed the dazed Webster. 'Ride up into the hills back of here. Hide yourself and the horses in a ravine until you're sure they've gone back to the village. Then come down and meet me here!'

'What's going to happen to you in the meantime?' Doc wanted to know.

'Don't worry! I'll make out!' Bart promised him, and gave the gray a slap on the flank that sent the Doc on his way with the two horses.

Bart watched until he was out of sight, quickly ran into the house and glanced around. There was a single stairway leading to the second floor; and in the kitchen at the rear a good-sized window facing the barn. He rushed out to the kitchen and, picking up a plain chair, hurled it through the window as if he were using it as an escape route. Then he turned and ran up the stairs. In the second floor bedroom there was a square opening with a wood panel in the ceiling that led to the attic and the storage space up there. It was all painted white to resemble the regular section of the ceiling.

He pulled a chair up and stood on it to push the wooden panel out of position. The open square left was terribly small, but somehow he would have to manage to get through it.

He moved the chair back against the wall and, standing on it again, leaped forward and

28

just managed to grasp the edge of the opening without leaving any tell-tale chair underneath. He swung for a moment, the sockets of his arms aching under the strain. Then clenching his teeth, he forced himself up so that his head and one arm were through the aperture. Now he had to wriggle the rest of his long body through and for once he was glad he was thin. The attic space was hot, dirty and filled with cobwebs, but he cared nothing about that. Before he replaced the wood panel to leave himself in almost complete darkness he spotted the second panel in the slanted roof above him, which was held in place by rusty bolts. This would give access to the slanting, shingled roof and the chimney.

He heard the sound of riders coming up into the yardway and the excited shouting of male voices. He carefully replaced the wooden panel and stretched out full length in his hiding place, his ear to the ceiling as he waited breathlessly to hear what would happen.

There were the sounds of heavy footsteps clumping through the house. And from somewhere below he heard a dialogue between the gruff-voiced Sheriff Hill and someone who spoke in a reedy whine.

'Kingstons are gone and so is he,' the whiner shouted.

'Through the kitchen window,' Sheriff Hill roared. 'He musta high-tailed it out the back

29

soon as he heard us comin'!'

'Which way would he go?' the whiny one wanted to know.

Sheriff Hill came clomping up the stairs. 'Better make sure he or one of the old folks ain't up here,' he said.

Bart held his breath as he heard the sheriff moving around below. But the panel must have escaped the sheriff's notice, for after a moment of silence he went on to the other room. Bart gave a sigh of relief.

From the stairs came the whiny voice. 'You see anything up there, Sheriff?'

The sheriff moved back to the stairs and started down. 'If I had, you'd have known it before this,' he declared in a disgusted rumble. 'The boys and I will spread out around the countryside with the horses for a search. You better stay here and stand guard.'

'You betcha, Sheriff,' the whiny voice agreed, apparently pleased at what he considered an easy job.

Next Bart heard the sheriff's gruff voice out by the barn giving orders, and then the sound of men shouting and the horses pounding off. All at once it became strangely quiet, so quiet Bart wondered if the decision to leave the whiny-voiced man on guard had been changed. He couldn't hear anyone at all below.

With great care to make no sound, he edged his way across the rafters and tried the bolt.

30

When he started to move it, there was an alarming squeal of metal on metal. The rusty bolt had not been opened in some time. He forced himself to slide it just the merest fraction and then wait. It was tedious and hot work in the dark inferno of the attic, which was now at its worst under the direct rays of the midday sun. At long last he freed the bolt and very gradually pushed against the wooden hatch.

When it was open a half-inch, he peered out to get a partial view of the area around the barn. He also gulped in some fresh air, for which he was grateful. There was no one in sight and, encouraged, he opened the hatch wider. Then he heard a sound from the front of the house and ducked inside again.

After a moment, a seedy-looking cowpoke came into sight, mounted on a big dark horse. There was a rifle across the rider's saddle, but the wizened face of the man showed him to be relaxed and not expecting anything to happen. Bart considered quickly. His next move would have to be the right one, or he'd only multiply his trouble or wind up a prisoner in Sheriff Hill's trap.

The cowpoke reined his mount to a halt just a few feet past Bart. Then he proceeded to take out the makings to roll himself a smoke. Bart watched him with fascinated eyes. It seemed a situation made to order.

Very gradually he opened the hatch, then

eased himself out on the hot shingles of the slanting roof until at last he was flat on his stomach, looking down at the slumped shoulders of the cowpoke as he sat rolling himself a cigarette. He measured the distance between himself and the man on the horse and saw that it was not too great. The moment he lifted himself and poised to jump down and tackle the cowpoke, he would give the alarm. It was a question of how quickly the man could grasp his rifle and turn it on him.

Bart felt he could wait no longer. With a swift intake of breath, he jumped up and dived down toward the startled rider. He grasped the cowpoke by the arms before he could put the rifle into use, and it clattered to the ground. The black horse whinnied and reared at Bart's unexpected impact on its back, and as the two men fell struggling, the big animal pranced and pounded around them, adding a new hazard. Once a heavy-shod foot came down past Bart's ear. He rolled over, only to see a hoof poised over his head again.

At the same time the reedy-voiced man was clawing and screaming with rage and giving Bart a hard fight. After a moment the horse ran off, and Bart was able to give his full attention to pummeling his opponent. A well directed blow to the chin finally put the wizened-faced man temporarily out of action. Bart found a piece of rope and bound him hand and foot.

Then he dragged him out of sight into the barn.

When he came out again, he saw no sign of the black horse. It had apparently taken fright and run off. He was stranded there without a mount. Except that he had his freedom, he wasn't much better off than before. Then he heard what had this morning become all too familiar a sound—approaching horses!

CHAPTER THREE

Bart ran back to the shelter of the barn to await developments.

The rider came into the yard, and Bart could have whooped of delight, for a perspiring Doc Webster was returning with the horses. Bart mounted his big bay without hesitation.

'Let's head for town, and fast,' he cried. 'How did you manage it so neatly?'

Doc Webster chuckled. 'Sheriff rode past me quarter of an hour ago. I figured it would be about right.'

'Let's go then,' Bart said, heading the bay for the road.

The two men said little as they rode the short distance into town. 'We'd best go direct to Mayor Peters place,' Doc said. 'You follow after me.'

Bart nodded. A few minutes later they were

33

on a street that paralleled the main one, and before a big house with a black sign that said, 'H. Peters, Undertaker.'

They dismounted, and the puffing Doc Webster led the way in, at the same time confiding to Bart, 'Another morning like this, and I might as well stay here and save him the trouble of picking me up somewhere.'

Bart found himself standing beside Doc Webster in a dingy office. At a desk sat a small, freakishly thin and white-skinned old man, who regarded them sourly over steel-rimmed spectacles.

'What is it?' he rasped in a low voice.

'Me and my friend want to see Mayor Peters,' Doc told the odd old man.

The oldster scowled and nodded toward a door at the end of the office. 'He's out back. You better go on out there if you want him.'

Doc Webster thanked the old man, who promptly went back to a study of the ledger before him, and beckoned Bart to follow him. They went out the rear door and down a narrow, dark corridor.

Doc chuckled and confided, 'That's Ezra Mullin, the mayor's clerk. Reckon he keeps him going with a shot of embalming fluid now and then.'

Suddenly they emerged through another door to find themselves in a big room with a high ceiling and an acrid smell. All around the walls on special shelves were piled coffins. Bart had never seen so many coffins in one spot.

And in the middle of the room stood a thin, stooped man with cadaverous features. He was working over a fancy oak casket set out on a table and only raised his eyes as they approached.

'Good morning, Mayor!' Doc Webster said with a forced heartiness that struck Bart as being out of place.

'Good morning to you, Doctor,' the man in the dark suit said soberly in a sepulchral tone. His sad eyes took in Bart questioningly. 'What brings you here?'

'I'm not looking for an early fitting in one of your wooden overcoats, if that's what you're thinking!' Doc Webster said, and laughed loudly at his own joke.

Mayor Peters did not even crack a smile. He held up a polishing cloth for them to observe and said, 'I promise you, you could do worse. I have a fine lot of caskets here. I've just been polishing the handles of this one. Solid oak! Came all the way from St. Louis.'

Doc Webster nodded. 'She's a dandy!'

Mayor Peters regarded it lovingly. 'A beautiful item for the proper person,' he said with a deep sigh. And then he raised his eyes to take in Bart again. 'Is it you who has come to do business with me, young man? I don't seem to recall you.'

35

Before Bart could answer, the doctor went over to the mayor and said, 'To tell you the truth, Mayor, this boy is in a spot of trouble, and I promised him you'd help him.'

Mayor Peters' bloodhound face showed a disconcerted expression. 'Wasn't that being a little previous, Doctor? I'm waiting for you to explain.'

'You bet!' Doc Webster said. 'This lad is Bart Landry, who has come here to visit the Kingstons.'

The mayor–undertaker showed interest. 'Ah, yes, the Kingstons! Very old and not too well. How is their health presently?' he asked Bart.

'They seemed fair enough when I last talked to them,' Bart said.

The sad-looking man raised his eyebrows. 'At their age you never can tell, though. Up one day, down the next! Believe me, I know the story well.'

Doc Webster was growing impatient and waved a hand to brush the topic aside. 'You'll get the Kingstons soon enough, Mayor. That is, providing you don't let their visitor here down. Bart got in a little trouble standing up for me in the Ace Saloon last night, and now Sheriff Hill has a trumped-up murder charge against him.'

'Would you mind explaining all this in detail?' Mayor Peters asked in his slow, sad way.

Doc immediately launched into a rapid but

36

full account of all that had taken place, and wound up by saying, 'As far as we know, the sheriff and his posse are right on our tails now!'

Mayor Peters sighed deeply and studied Bart with somber eyes. 'You have indeed gotten yourself into a lot of trouble, young man. But it may cheer you to know that any hanging victim in Durez City is assured of a decent burial, paid for by the town and carefully supervised by me.'

'Dang it, Mayor!' Doc sputtered angrily. 'There isn't no consolation in a proper funeral! I want you to see Bart gets a fair hearing.'

The mayor raised his eyebrows again as if the doctor's directness had scandalized him. He addressed himself to Bart. 'This fight between you and Clancy Evans happened just as Doc has outlined it?'

'Yes,' Bart said, feeling they had made a mistake in appealing to this eccentric for aid.

'And Clancy Evans was the one pulled the knife on you and began the brawl?'

'He came at me from the alley.'

The mayor nodded. 'And you used no weapons against him other than your bare fists, and he was alive to the best of your knowledge when you left him in the gutter?'

'Yes to both questions, Mayor,' Bart said. 'I didn't know he was dead until Doc came out to the Kingston place and told me.'

Doc Webster nodded vigorously. 'He was

proper surprised. I could tell.'

'I don't see why you should have anything to fear,' the mayor said. 'When Sheriff Hill shows up, I'll see that a jury is picked and a proper inquest held.'

'If you'll do that, sir,' Bart said, 'I don't think they can prove I did anything wrong.'

'You bet they can't!' Doc said indignantly. 'Clancy's head was broken when he hit that rock by accident. Bart didn't mean to kill him.'

'Perhaps it might be wise for you to remain here for a time,' the mayor said, 'if you're both so sure sheriff Hill and his hot-headed group are following you.'

Doc Webster nodded. 'Good idea, Mayor. I have a hunch they're not more than ten minutes or so behind us. And when they spot our horses outside, they'll likely be paying this place a call.'

The mayor blinked mournfully. 'My own conclusion.' He turned to Bart. 'Your late opponent, Clancy Evans, has come my way, of course. I fitted him with an elegant mahogany job which Jim Malone will pay for. He's resting in state in a back room of the Ace Saloon. You should drop by and see him. I did some lovely work on his bruises.'

'I'll take your word for it, Mayor,' Bart said with a grim expression. 'I saw enough of Clancy Evans when he was alive.'

The discussion was ended by the sound of

loud voices in the office outside. Bart recognized one of them as belonging to Sheriff Hill. He gave Doc Webster a knowing look. But the veteran merely glanced at the mayor with a grin on his mottled face.

'Sounds like our visitors have arrived,' he said.

'Indeed it does,' the mayor acknowledged, and to Bart's surprise at once went back to polishing the handles of the oak coffin.

The stamping of feet and murmur of voices gradually came nearer in the corridor. Then the door burst open and Sheriff Hill marched into the big, shadowy room with his Colt drawn and ready to use.

He glared at Bart. 'I reckoned you'd be in here.'

Bart smiled at him thinly. 'That didn't take much figuring, Sheriff. I left my horse outside where you could see it. I'm not in hiding.'

Sheriff Hill kept him covered with the Colt and spoke to the mayor. 'I'm taking this cowpoke in for the murder of Clancy Evans,' he announced.

The mayor stopped and looked up mildly. 'I think there has been a mistake, Sheriff.'

The burly sheriff's square face set in a scowl. 'What kind of crazy talk is that?' he asked the mayor defiantly.

The mayor came around in front of the casket with a doleful look on the bloodhound face.

'I've heard a different version of Clancy's death,' he said. He waved a hand toward Bart. 'This young man contends it happened in a fair fight and was an accident.'

Sheriff Hill's eyes narrowed. 'The boys will tell you different. He was rowin' with Clancy in the Ace Saloon and finally got him when he went outside.'

'The matter will be settled at a proper inquest,' Mayor Peters said calmly, revealing a power of authority Bart hadn't suspected. 'We'll hold it tonight at the City Hall. Until then this young man will be free on his own recognizance.'

The sheriff's associates looked startled and began to mumble among themselves. Sheriff Hill rubbed his chin uncertainly with his free hand.

'You don't know what you're doin', Mayor,' he complained, 'allowing this killer to go loose. He'll skip town right off!'

'I'm perfectly willing to face an inquest,' Bart spoke up.

The sheriff gave him a disgusted glance and appealed to the mayor. 'This is your last word on the matter, Mayor?'

Mayor Peters nodded. 'That's it.'

Sheriff Hill slid the Colt back in its holster and stood uncertainly for a moment, clearly angry at being put in his place before the assorted hoodlums he'd gathered to form his posse.

'If it weren't for the good of the town, I'd offer you back my badge, Mayor,' he said. 'You ain't got no right to mess in the affairs of the law!'

'As the head of the town, it seems to me I have every right,' Mayor Peters told him. 'You can schedule the inquest for eight o'clock and round up a jury of six.'

'Who is going to preside?' the sheriff wanted to know.

Mayor Peters' bloodhound face turned toward Doc Webster, who had been standing by silently, taking it all in. He said, 'Doc Webster is still the official coroner of Durez City as far as I know. Naturally he'll be in charge.'

The sheriff glowered. 'I might have known,' he sputtered. 'Those two galoots are as thick as thieves. They ganged up on Clancy Evans in the Ace Saloon.' He continued to glare at Bart and Doc Webster.

The doctor's mottled face wore a wise grin. 'Still, Sheriff, you must admit your own action exposed the device Clancy was using to cheat at cards.'

'I ain't denying any of that,' the sheriff protested.

Mayor Peters sighed. 'Gentlemen, it seems to me we're prolonging this discussion far beyond the point of good sense. We'll settle everything this evening at the inquest.'

The sheriff wheeled around and herded out his motley gang of cowhands. At the same time he murmured loudly enough for them all to hear about the desirability of Durez City soon acquiring the services of another and more expert undertaker.

When they had gone, Mayor Peters turned to Bart and Doc Webster with an expression of dismay that was almost comic. 'You heard that criticism,' he said dolefully. 'And it is my pride I turn out the most life-like corpses in the State.'

Doc Webster chuckled. 'That was just a case of sour grapes, Mayor. The sheriff was sore because you didn't let him string up Bart and bring him to you as another customer.'

'An extremely rude person, the sheriff,' Mayor Peters commented. And then, giving Doc a sharp glance: 'I suggest you shave and clean up before the inquest. It is important the presiding authority have the required dignity.'

Doc Webster blinked his bloodshot eyes. 'Depend on it, Mayor.'

'I will,' the mayor said, and turned to Bart. 'I have given you a fair chance to state your case, young man. I will count on you presenting yourself at the proper time and not trying to run off.'

Bart's thin face was sober. 'I'll be there, sir,' he promised.

'Then that settles things,' the mayor said, and turned to go back to his polishing. Doc Webster nudged Bart with an elbow, indicating it was time they left. They did so without a word.

Outside, Doc Webster looked at Bart and said, 'Well, what did you think of His Honor?'

Bart shrugged. 'Odd as they come. But underneath that peculiar surface there's a sharp person. The people in Durez City made no mistake when they elected him.'

'He's the only one Jim Malone and his slippery crowd don't own,' the old doctor told him. 'They let the mayor win because they thought he was a kind of a comic candidate. But it turns out the joke is on them. He happens to be honest.'

'I hope he can keep order at the inquest,' Bart worried as he took the reins of the bay and prepared to get into the saddle.

'Don't worry about that. He'll be there and see things are done proper. The big problem will be the jury. Since Sheriff Hill has the right to call them, you can be sure he'll pick his own men.'

'I'll take my chances,' Bart said. 'Right now I want to pick up some food. Provisions are kind of light out at the Kingstons'.' He mounted the bay.

Doc Webster clambered up on the thin gray and said, 'We can go around by the grocery and

43

then on to my place.' He paused and shot Bart a queer look. 'Did you say the Kingstons had gone off somewhere?'

'That's right,' Bart said brusquely.

'Something new for them!'

'So I understand,' the tall stranger agreed in an expressionless voice. The two men headed their horses toward the main street at a slow walk.

Bart spent some time in the big general store. He picked up canned milk and a lot of other canned foods that would keep and come in handy during the days ahead.

The doctor's house was on the other side of the main street. His sign was still out, but badly in need of paint, as were the house itself and the once-white picket fence surrounding it. The grounds were grown with grass and weeds, and at first glance the place gave the impression of being abandoned. The inside was almost as badly neglected.

The old doctor bustled ahead of Bart and tried to clear the messy table up a little. He smiled apologetically over his shoulder. 'Don't take too close a look around here. Been batching it a long while.'

Bart promised he wouldn't and settled down in the squalor. Meanwhile, the doctor found his shaving kit and settled down to remove his rubble of gray beard.

A shave and a wash did miracles for the

44

doctor. From somewhere he brought out a fresh white shirt and a black string tie. By the time he'd changed and brushed off his coat and trousers, he looked a little more like a real professional man and not so much like a broken-down drunk.

Studying himself in a piece of broken mirror stuck in place above the sink, he said, 'I reckon I'll suggest the proper authority now.'

'A little soap and water can make a big difference in a man,' Bart said, nodding his approval.

'You know a girl called Eve Driscoll?'

The mottled face took on a smile. 'Sure. Pretty little thing.'

'She called on me just before you came this morning. Seems she has been helping the Kingstons.'

'Sounds like Eve,' the doctor agreed. 'And she is as near as anyone to their place. Her father owns all the land above them. Has a big ranch. Colonel Driscoll has made the Lazy T one of the best paying outfits in these parts.'

'So he's a military man?' Bart asked.

'Confederate army,' Doc Webster said. 'Lost an arm at Gettysburg. Came here afterward and bought the Lazy T, which was pretty well run down then. Eve was just a tot. He brought her up with a housekeeper, hefty old Mexican gal, and when she was old enough sent her to one of those fancy boarding schools for girls in New England.'

'I thought she had an Eastern accent,' Bart acknowledged.

The doctor nodded. 'She's a real lady now, and smart as a whip, just like the colonel. Not many put anything over on him.'

'She seemed a little upset to find me at the house and the Kingstons gone,' Bart said.

Doc Webster eyed him with curiosity. 'Well, don't you think that's natural?'

Bart's pale blue eyes held a touch of annoyance as he stared at the battered old doctor. 'No. Can't say that I do,' he drawled.

The old doctor showed confusion. 'Son, I'm not trying to say there's anything wrong. But you'll find folks are going to ask questions!'

'So it seems,' Bart said dryly.

'The Kingstons are old and sick. Haven't moved from that place in years. Then you come along, and they're gone before the next dawn, without a word to anyone!'

'On a visit to their nephew in Santa Ana,' Bart said.

'I didn't know they had a nephew.'

'They've got a couple.'

The doctor frowned. 'You one of them?'

Bart shook his head. 'No blood relation. Just a friend.'

'Well, I guess it's their business and yours,' the doctor admitted with a shrug. 'But you shouldn't feel upset about Eve Driscoll being

· 46

worried about those two old people. She means well.'

'I'm sure of that.'

'I better rustle us up something to eat,' the old man said unhappily, apparently knowing nothing would be gained by pursuing the subject but still not satisfied in his own mind. 'Guess it'll have to be beans and hard-tack.'

The meal wasn't fancy, but Bart was hungry enough to enjoy any kind of food. Afterward he helped Doc Webster clean up the kitchen, and then they started out for the inquest.

The City Hall was a square frame building that Doc Webster told him served not only as the seat of civic affairs, but also as a courthouse and church on occasion. It was also used by the rare traveling theatrical companies that came to the little town. For this reason it was fitted with a stage that rose several feet above the main section of the plank floor of the interior, and there was a draw curtain.

A number of men stood outside, and there were horses and carriages hitched to posts.

Doc Webster led Bart through the curious group and into the cool interior of the building. Quite a few were already seated in the auditorium section, and on the stage Sheriff Hill was standing in earnest conversation with a deputy. There was a table and chair at the center, and six chairs for the jury set out at one side of the stage, with a single one for witnesses

47

at the other.

'We'll want another chair for you. Have it set next to my table,' the doctor whispered as they made their way down a side aisle.

Sheriff Hill became aware of their arrival and glared at them. Then he said something in a low voice to his deputy, who immediately went off somewhere.

The sheriff turned his back to them as they mounted the stage. A moment later the deputy returned with an extra chair, and Doc Webster directed him to place it on the right of the table. The doctor and Bart took their places.

It seemed the almost empty building filled completely within a few minutes of their arrival. Mayor Peters, dressed completely in black and solemn-faced, came to the stage and conferred first with Sheriff Hill and then with the doctor.

'You about ready, Doc?' he wanted to know.

'Any time you say, Mayor,' the old man agreed. He had removed his hat and was mopping his brow. Bart decided he was perspiring from nerves rather than the heat. The building was cool.

The six jurors filed in and studied Bart with suspicious eyes. He was sure the sheriff had picked the half-dozen hardest heads in town and abandoned the little hope he'd entertained of being fairly heard.

Doc Webster got the inquest under way. He told briefly of being with the sheriff when the body of Clancy Evans was found. Sheriff Hill stood at one end of the stage, scowling, as the facts were recited.

At the end of Doc Webster's account, there was a rustle in the front row and the mayor stood up and turned his bloodhound features toward the sheriff. He said, 'May I address a question to you, Sheriff Hill? How does it happen Clancy Evans was free at the time of his death? It is my understanding that you took him into custody at the time you found him cheating in the Ace Saloon.'

Sheriff Hill's square face took on a crimson hue. He cleared his throat and said importantly, 'I let Clancy go on the promise he would leave town. That is what we generally do with small-time crooks. He'd given back the money he won by cheating in the poker game. I figured things would be squared if he made himself scarce.'

Mayor Peters looked more doleful than ever. 'It seems you took a good deal on yourself without consultation. Clancy is dead because you freed him to engage in a brawl.'

CHAPTER FOUR

It was a good point, and Bart glanced quickly in the direction of the six men on the jury and saw

49

that it had not been missed by them. A murmur of reaction went through the crowded building.

Sheriff Hill recovered himself to say, 'I didn't expect a murderer was waiting for him when I let him go.'

'But he did promise to leave town at once when you released him?' the mayor asked.

'He sure did,' the sheriff said uneasily, looking as if he expected another trap to close on him.

It did. The mayor said calmly, 'It seems he didn't stick to his word, but instead waited to waylay Bart Landry.'

'Maybe it was the other way around,' the sheriff protested. 'Clancy might have been on his way to the livery stable when this stranger caught up with him.' He emphasized the word stranger and jerked his head toward Bart.

Doc Webster cleared his throat. 'I suggest it is time we heard from Landry and the other witnesses.'

Mayor Peters nodded and resumed his seat. Doc Webster handled the situation well. He had several witnesses relate what had taken place in the saloon and then describe the scene when the body was found later. At last he called on Bart to tell his story.

That just about wound up matters. The foreman of the jury asked a few questions, and then he and his companions retired to the wings of the stage to decide on their verdict. When it came, Bart was pleasantly surprised. The jury found that Clancy Evans had met his death through misadventure as the result of a street brawl. They recommended that no one be held accountable.

The doctor picked up his papers from the desk. 'That calls for a drink!' He grasped Bart by the arm; ignoring the scowling sheriff, they left the stage and went down to the level of the auditorium.

They had gone only a few steps when they were abruptly confronted by a lovely young woman in an expensive gray suit with a wide flowing skirt and wearing the briefest of matching hats on the side of her blonde head. Her hair was styled in an upsweep, and she had roguish blue eyes and a knowing smile.

She held out a tiny hand. 'Congratulations, Mr. Landry,' she said in a low, pleasing voice. 'I'm sure the jury acted as they should.'

He accepted the tiny hand, a little puzzled. And he was more perplexed by the manner in which the roguish blue eyes lingered on him.

'Thanks,' he said quietly.

'You've only just come to Durez City?' the girl said.

'That's right, miss,' he said quietly.

'I guessed that,' she said. 'I'd have remembered if I'd seen you before. You are not going to let this small unpleasantness scare you away, I trust.'

51

'No.' He shook his head. 'I aim to stay awhile.'

The girl continued to stare at him with rapt attention. 'I'm glad to hear that,' she said. 'We need a man of your type in Durez City.'

It was a strange statement, coming from this girl he'd never seen until a few minutes before. Bart smiled. 'You reckon you know my type?'

'Of course!' she said. 'I had only to watch you on the stage while you told your story just now. I could tell you have courage and the ability to take care of yourself.' She flashed a smile in Doc Webster's direction. 'Not that the doctor and mayor didn't do very well by you.'

'Thanks, Miss,' Doc Webster said politely. 'Fact is, since Bart here was innocent, it wasn't any big task.'

'It could have gone differently,' the blonde girl said. 'Clancy Evans deserved what happened to him. He'd been looking for trouble for just ages. I felt that I wanted to stand up and shout out some of the things I knew about him.'

Bart was impressed by her spirit and startled by her frankness. He said, 'I am glad to hear somebody else felt he wasn't a saint.'

'Lots of people here tonight knew the truth,' she said. 'But not many are able to stand up to the crowd that run this town. That's why I say it is good you've come here, Mr. Landry. And I hope you decide to stay.'

52

Doc Webster winked at her. 'Depend on me to keep him here awhile, Maggie.'

'I will,' she said. And looking at Bart, she asked, 'Where are you staying?'

'The Kingston place,' he said.

She nodded. 'On the outskirts of town. I know it.' The smile returned to her pretty face. 'We must talk some more, Mr. Landry. Maybe I'll take a ride out that way soon.'

Before Bart could think of a suitable reply, a new figure appeared on the scene. A broad-shouldered, swarthy young man with a handsome if somewhat weak face came up beside the girl. Bart could see by his clothes he was probably a prosperous rancher or the son of one. He wore several rings on his fingers, one an oversize diamond, and there was a beaded band around the crown of his light-colored sombrero. His six-shooter, in its hand-tooled holster, had mother-of-pearl stocks. And the neckerchief at his throat was of bright yellow silk.

He took the girl's arm and addressed her with a smooth insolence. 'You sure like to waste time chattering, Maggie. Didn't you know I was outside waiting for you?'

'I knew,' she said easily. 'I just wasn't in a hurry.'

'Well, you are now, honey,' he said, tugging at her arm. 'We got places to go and things to do.'

53

'I don't know about you,' the blonde girl said sharply, 'but I'm going straight home, Nick.'

He laughed. 'We'll see about that.' He pulled on her arm again.

The blonde girl lingered long enough to smile over her shoulder at Bart and say, 'I'll see you soon, Mr. Landry.'

Then the dandified Nick led her to the door with him.

Bart watched the two go out. 'Who is he?' he asked.

'Nick Cressy, foreman of the Diamond O,' Doc Webster said. 'He runs the ranch for Jim Malone. And don't let those trick clothes fool you. He's hard and he's nasty.'

'Who is this Maggie?' Bart demanded.

The old man wore a rueful smile. 'I reckon you won't believe me. She's Jim Malone's daughter.'

'Jim Malone's daughter!'

Doc Webster nodded. 'She and Jim don't see things eye to eye,' the old man told him confidentially. 'Her mother was a singer in the saloon. When Maggie was three years old, she ran off with a traveling show actor and left the kid here for Jim to bring up. She never came back. Word around is she died back East some time ago. Anyway, Maggie grew up hating her father and blaming him for what happened.'

'But she lives at the ranch with him?'

Doc nodded. 'Sure. She takes everything she

can but gives nothing in return. No affection and no loyalty. Jim always treated her mother like dirt until she ran away, and now Maggie is paying him back.'

'Not a pretty story,' Bart said. 'She can't be a very happy girl.'

'I reckon you're right,' the old man agreed. 'Of course her Dad wants her to marry Nick Cressy, and that is enough to make her sure she won't.' He grinned. 'Let's go latch onto that drink.'

They resumed their walk to the door. Bart gave the old man a sour smile. 'I suppose that is why she used me to tantalize this Nick,' he said. 'It's one of her ways of getting at him.'

Dusk was closing in as they stepped outside. The yard, that had been so filled with loiterers when they arrived, was empty now. They headed for their own horses as a carriage came rolling into the cleared area, raising a cloud of dust.

Bart turned but for a moment was not able clearly to make out who was sitting on the seat of the vehicle. Then as it drew close he saw that Eve Driscoll held the reins. At her side was a white-haired man, wearing a dark Stetson and a suit with the left arm empty and shoved into his coat pocket.

The pretty girl who'd been to see him at the ranch that morning drew the reins tight, and the carriage came to a halt. The white-haired man was on the side nearest them and leaned over to greet Doc Webster.

'Good evening, Doctor,' he said in a voice whose soft accent betrayed his Southern origin.

'Evenin', Colonel Driscoll,' the doctor said, indicating Bart with a gesture. 'This is a newcomer to town, Bart Landry.'

The colonel eyed him coldly. 'I believe he and my daughter have met. I wanted to be here for the inquest, but we didn't quite make it. I take it this young man was cleared of any complicity in Clancy Evans' death.'

'That's right, sir,' Bart said.

The colonel went on: 'You are staying at the Kingstons' place?'

Bart nodded. 'Yes.'

'My daughter tells me they've disappeared.'

'Gone to visit their nephew,' Bart corrected him.

There was open doubt on the colonel's aristocratic features. He said, 'My daughter seems to think there is something strange about the whole business.'

Bart gave a shrug. 'I'm afraid I can't help that.'

Colonel Driscoll regarded him bleakly. 'I want you to know, young man, we're not finished looking into this. You'll hear from me again. It seems you've managed to get into a good deal of trouble since arriving in Durez City!' He turned to his daughter. 'It is pointless

56

to waste any more time on him.' And to the doctor, 'Good night, Doctor.'

Eve flashed Bart a woeful glance as she gave the horses a free rein and the carriage creaked off into the growing darkness. Doc Webster gazed after them with a dismayed look on his mottled face.

'You got Eve and her old man upset pretty bad,' he said.

Bart made a move toward his horse. 'They are the ones causing the trouble.'

The old doctor shook his head. 'I don't know, Bart. I think you could have been a bit more civil to them. You just got out of this trouble by the skin of your teeth, and now you're headed for more.'

Bart mounted the bay. 'If that's the way it has to be, then that's the way it has to be.'

The doctor didn't answer, but got on the mangy gray, and they both rode back toward the business section of the town.

Doc Webster reined up the gray and indicated the lights of a building just ahead. 'We better go in here tonight,' he said. 'It's the Round Barrel Saloon. There might be some touchy folks at the Ace, with Clancy still in one of the back rooms.'

'Whatever you think,' Bart agreed.

Doc found them a place at the crowded bar and ordered a double brandy for himself and a whiskey for Bart. Then he turned to him and asked, 'What do you plan on next?'

'I'm going back to the Kingstons' place.'

Doc's mottled face looked a shade uncomfortable. 'Might be just as well for you to keep away from there for a few days. You heard what the colonel said. Why don't you stay in town and bunk with me?'

Bart shook his head. 'No good.'

Their drinks came, they had downed them, and Bart turned to leave. As he did he came face to face with a big, swarthy man with beady eyes, thin lips and a scar on his right cheekbone.

The man uttered a quick oath. 'Texas Jack!'

Bart looked at him with a stony expression. 'What did you say?'

The big man looked uneasy. 'I guess I made a mistake. I thought I knew you.'

'That was a bad mistake,' Bart said, his pale blue eyes fixed on the beady ones of the other. 'I never saw you before.'

The big man had turned sallow. 'I guess I've been drinking too much. I should have known better.'

Bart nodded. 'Satisfied?'

'Sure!' the big man said. 'Sorry, stranger!' And he moved on to the other end of the bar, pausing once to glance back apprehensively at Bart. Then he was lost in the crowd.

Doc Webster was at Bart's elbow now. 'Seemed to think he knew you.'

58

Bart looked at the shorter man and saw a strange knowing expression on his mottled, purplish face. He said, 'It happens all the time in places like this. People come up and think you're somebody else.'

Doc Webster's bloodshot eyes met his. 'He seemed pretty sure at first.'

'They always are. He soon found out his mistake.'

'Found out he wasn't wise,' the doctor corrected him.

Bart regarded him with a thin smile of distaste. 'You heard him say he was wrong.'

'But he acted mighty funny just the same.'

'I can't account for his behavior. I just set him straight.'

'He called you Texas Jack.'

'Did he?' Bart was unconcerned.

The doctor nodded. 'I heard him. No mistake about that. You know who Texas Jack is?'

'You forget,' Bart said, 'I'm a stranger in this part of the country.'

'So you are,' Doc Webster said. 'So you wouldn't know he's an outlaw wanted all through the south–west for train robbery and murder. Repeated a half-dozen times, so the reward posters say.'

Bart's expression was blank. 'You've seen the posters?'

59

The old man nodded. 'Every post office has one.'

'What does this Texas Jack look like?'

'Nobody knows,' Doc Webster said with a wise smile. 'But I've heard he is a tall, thin man. He paused. 'Like you.'

Bart nodded. 'That could explain our friend's error.'

'You leaving now?'

'I'm on my way.'

He stepped out into the darkness and started toward the place where he had left the bay. He hadn't gone five steps when he felt the muzzle of a gun pressed against his spine.

A low voice said, 'Walk, mister, fast and quiet like! You and me have things to talk about!' Bart recognized it as belonging to the man who had called him Texas Jack.

CHAPTER FIVE

Bart walked along the deserted wooden sidewalk in the darkness, his eyes fixed straight ahead as he tried to figure out what his best move would be.

They were moving away from the regular buildings now and coming to a deserted end of the secondary street. Ahead loomed the shadowy shapes of what Bart took to be a couple of deserted shacks. The gun at his back

60

prodded him on.

The beady-eyed man whispered, 'To the right, *señor*. The space between the buildings!'

Bart obeyed the man's instructions, and as they left the sidewalk for the hard, uneven ground, their pace slackened. This was to be the spot where their differences would be settled.

'Far enough, *Señor* Texas Jack,' his captor said with a harsh chuckle.

'You're making a bad mistake,' Bart argued.

'You are the one making the mistake, *señor*,' the man said, pressing the gun even more tightly against him. 'You did not deceive me.'

'I'm not Texas Jack!'

'We will waste no time,' the man snapped in his ear. 'You know what it is I am after.'

Bart decided to try playing along with him. 'And if I do talk?'

'We'll decide that later,' the beady-eyed one said.

'This is what you want to know,' Bart said, measuring his words slowly. And then he risked everything by snapping a hand around quickly and knocking the gun from the other's startled grasp.

The beady-eyed man let out a loud oath as the gun clattered on to the hard ground. Bart's left hand came up with decisive force and landed solidly on the jaw of his oversize opponent. The big man staggered back, tripped

61

on his spurs and landed in a heap. He rose quickly again with a snarl of hate and made a lunge for Bart's throat.

He dodged swiftly and lashed out hard with a left and then a right. The first blow hit the big man's chest, and the second landed on his face with a loud pulpy smack that caused him to reel backward. Bart was quick to follow his advantage and close in on the big man with a rapid rain of blows to his face and head.

The beady-eyed man groaned, and his right hand reached swiftly in a sudden move. Bart was aware of the quick gesture and a moment later caught the gleam of a wicked-looking long knife in the big man's grasp. With a wild cry he plunged forward, the blade narrowly missing Bart. The big man tried again, and this time Bart caught his arm and, using a professional wrestler's move, twisted it into a position where the extreme leverage threatened to snap it. The big man moaned out in anguish and let the knife slip from his fingers. But Bart did not ease the pressure; he bore down on the arm until it cracked.

The moment the bone snapped, the beady-eyed man gave another pitiful moan and slumped into unconsciousness. Breathing heavily and bruised and torn from the short, bitter struggle, Bart groped on the ground until he found his Stetson and the six-shooter belonging to his attacker. Then he ran back to the sidewalk and didn't slacken his pace until he reached the bay at the hitching post, mounted it and rode off toward the Kingston place.

Next morning he had a cut above one eye to remind him his encounter with the stranger in the darkness had really happened.

He could only hope the beady-eyed man would move on out of town after he had come to and had his arm looked after. In this way there would be no talk caused by the incident. The less the better, as far as he was concerned. To make it especially dangerous, the big man had called him Texas Jack within earshot of perhaps a dozen people.

Heading the bay in the direction from which Eve Driscoll had come the previous day, he let it canter along at a pleasant pace. He was soon riding through a series of foothills. Far behind towered the mountains. Already he felt better and was glad he'd made up his mind to take the ride. Then he came to large groups of Hereford cattle bearing the Lazy T brand. Here it was good grazing country.

All at once he saw a horse and rider coming over a ridge and heading toward him. It was only a moment later he recognized Eve Driscoll on her chestnut.

The pretty girl's soft brown hair was streaming in the breeze as she rode up. There was a look of mild astonishment on her face.

63

She reined the chestnut as she came even with him.

'I didn't expect to find you up here,' she said.

'I had a yen to ride,' he replied. 'I didn't realize how far I'd strayed on your property until I saw the brand on the cattle.'

She eyed him with open curiosity, but he had an intuitive feeling she was not so hostile as on the previous day or even the night before. She said, 'You know, I find you a puzzling person.'

He smiled. 'Why?'

She stroked the chestnut's mane gently, still watching him. 'I want very much to dislike you, and yet somehow I can't.'

Bart's pale blue eyes held a twinkle. 'That's promising.'

'I mean you don't seem the sort of person I suspect you are,' she said. 'But then I suppose that is why you might manage to get away with a good deal of villainy.'

'You're suggesting my peculiar charm puts people at a disadvantage in judging me,' he said in a bantering tone.

'I suppose so,' she admitted with a sigh. Her lovely brown eyes searched his face anxiously. 'You haven't really done something awful to the Kingstons, have you?'

'If I had, do you think I'd continue to stay on at their place as I have?'

She considered this. 'Not by all the normal rules. But then if you were a—' She stopped as

64

if she could not bring herself to say the word, and with some confusion began again. 'If you were a really dangerous person, you might be clever enough to brazen things out that way.'

Bart couldn't help admiring her clear thinking, even though it put him in a nasty spot. This girl would not be easy to deceive at any time. And her concern for the old couple had made her give particular attention to the problem of their disappearance.

He shrugged. 'I see I'll have to omit any arguments and rely only on my charm.'

'It might be the wise way.' She sighed.

'What is your father's opinion of me?' he asked her.

She gave the restless chestnut its head and circled out and back to him again. 'You shook his belief in my theories last night. He's almost convinced I'm making a lot of fuss about nothing. He told me so this morning.'

'An example of male shrewdness,' Bart joked, trying to conceal his satisfaction at the news.

He said, 'I'm glad you have decided not to let your imagination run away with you.'

Eve dazzled him with another of her lovely smiles. She wheeled the chestnut around to face the ridge again. 'Wouldn't you like to see some more of our place?' she asked.

'Very much,' he said. 'But I don't want to impose on you.'

'I'd enjoy showing you,' she said. 'What are

65

you anyway? A cowpoke?'

He shook his head. 'If I told you I was, you'd naturally decide I was a rustler.'

Eve laughed. 'Why do you say that?'

'You're determined always to think the worst about me.'

'I think you're terribly evasive,' she said. 'You didn't answer my question. What do you do for a living?'

'I used to work for the railway,' he said carefully.

She looked at him with an arched eyebrow. 'I'm not impressed. You're avoiding a direct answer again.'

He shrugged. 'Now I'm just traveling.'

'You don't have to tell me,' she said. And then, with a glance back, she called out: 'Follow me over the ridge. Then you'll be able to get a view of the ranch house.'

She let the chestnut go, and it bounded across the field and up the hill, moving gracefully under her. It made a pretty picture. Bart followed on the bay, and within a few moments the two riders were together again on the crest of the ridge. From there you could see the broad valley below and, far to the end of it, the buildings of the Lazy T. Doc Webster had not exaggerated when he had said it was quite a spread! The ranch house alone was as large and impressive as any he'd ever seen.

Eve Driscoll gave him a questioning glance. 'You like it?'

He nodded. 'Some place.'

'Dad has put his whole life into it.'

'I guess perhaps it was worth-while,' Bart admitted. 'It must be the biggest outfit in this area.'

She smiled. 'It is. Dad seldom goes into Durez City or takes any part in its affairs.'

He studied her shrewdly. 'No?'

'He doesn't approve of what is going on in there. On our own place we can live decently and avoid the ugliness Malone and his henchmen are bringing to this country.'

Bart's eyes narrowed. He studied the rich spread of the Lazy T. 'I'd like to be able to agree with you on that, but I can't.'

Fear showed for an instant in the lovely face. 'What do you mean?'

He crossed his hands on the saddle horn. 'What you call the ugliness is bound to extend if men like your father don't take their proper share of responsibility. In the end it will hit the Lazy T, and you'll find yourselves unable to fight it.'

'Dad lost most of his illusions in the war, along with his arm,' she said in a quiet voice. 'Now all he asks is that we be able to live our lives here in peace.'

He said, 'I reckon I should be heading back. It has been fun meeting you, Miss Driscoll.'

'Eve will do,' she told him, turning the

67

chestnut around to watch him as he prepared to go.

'Thanks, Eve,' he said with a smile. 'Just as long as you remember I'm Bart.'

She responded at once. 'Bart,' she said, 'there is nothing wrong at the Kingstons', is there?'

His forehead furrowed. 'Why do you keep asking me that?'

'I worry about those two old people. They were my friends, and I haven't many.'

He touched a hand to his Stetson in a gesture of farewell and gave her one of his mysterious looks. 'Seems to me women are always wanting to worry about something,' he said.

As he came close to the Kingston place, Bart suddenly reined the bay and stared at a horse tethered out by the barn. It took him only a moment to recognize it as the gray belonging to Doc Webster. So the Doc had made good on his promise and come out to see him. He jogged the bay into a trot again and continued on to the white frame house.

He got down from the bay, and Doc Webster came over to greet him. The old man looked as if he might have been drinking again. There was a fresh crop of gray stubble on his bloated face, and his eyes were red as he squinted at Bart in the bright sunshine.

'I've been waiting for you,' he said.

'So I see.'

'You don't appear too glad to see me,' Doc

Webster said, exposing yellowed teeth in a grin.

'I'm not set up for visitors here,' Bart replied, and led the bay into the barn.

Doc Webster followed him and stood leaning in the doorway. He said, 'The Kingstons haven't gotten back yet?'

'Not yet.' Bart busied himself with the bay.

'I figured not,' the old man said. 'You expecting them soon?'

'When they come.'

Doc Webster chuckled. 'That way you're bound not to be disappointed.'

Bart came out from the bay's stall and stood facing him in the doorway of the barn. 'Is that what you came out here for? To ask about the Kingstons?'

'One of the things,' the old man said, giving him a wise look.

'And what are your other reasons?'

'I wanted to tell you how busy I've been.'

Bart's eyebrows raised. 'Busy? You?'

Doc Webster stood up straight and drew his shabby coat around him with some dignity. 'You think that's so strange?'

Bart nodded. 'Considering you do most of your doctoring in bars these days.'

A hurt expression crossed the mottled face. 'I'll overlook that remark,' Doc Webster said, 'seeing that it comes from a friend.'

'You're straining that friendship, coming out here with a lot of questions about the

Kingstons,' Bart said impatiently. 'I asked you to stay away.'

'I missed you, Bart,' the old man said. 'I don't have many people to talk to these days.'

Bart noted the appealing expression on the doctor's face and felt a little sorry for him. 'I enjoy your company too, you old coot,' he said, 'but in the right place and at the time. I intended to ride into town tonight, and we could have met then for a chat.'

Doc Webster beamed. 'Now you sound more like yourself.' He paused. 'I tell you, Bart, things are happening in Durez City. And Jim Malone and the sheriff are stirring up a lot of talk about you.'

Bart frowned. 'Still?'

'Sure. You beat them last night. You don't think they're going to take it without striking back? Jim and the sheriff aren't used to being licked.'

'What are they saying now?'

'Hinting about what is going on out here,' Doc Webster said. 'They're saying you're some no-account relative of the Kingstons who knew they had money and came out here and killed them for it.'

Bart managed a cold laugh. 'Everyone knows the Kingstons don't have anything!'

Doc looked worried. 'Maybe. But some people remember the old man did some gold mining back a few years. He thought he had a

70

rich vein, and then it dried right up.'

'So?'

'Now they think maybe the mine didn't turn out poor after all; that old man Kingston might have dug himself out a good supply of nuggets and stored them away somewhere; and that you knew about it and came here to get them.'

Bart's bony face went grim. 'Fits, doesn't it?' he asked with sarcasm.

'The way they tell it, it does.' Doc licked his swollen lips and waited to hear what he'd say next.

Bart said, 'Just now I was talking with Eve Driscoll up at her place. If anyone should know the truth about the Kingstons, she should. She helped them enough. And she's convinced they were dirt poor!'

Doc showed interest. 'You been talking to Eve?'

He nodded. 'That's where I came from.'

The old man winked knowingly. 'I tell you, Bart, you know how to get around the ladies. Now I'd say that Maggie Malone was some interested in you last night. And this morning it's little Eve! SHe ain't mad at you any more?'

'She realizes how ridiculous her suspicions were,' Bart said.

'Well!' Doc showed surprise. 'And she knows the Kingstons still haven't showed up?'

'People who go on vacations don't return in a couple of days,' Bart said firmly. 'Even you

71

should realize that.'

'Guess you're right, Bart,' the old man said apologetically. 'But we got clear off the track. I was just about to tell you that I've been busy as coroner again.'

Bart eyed him. 'You have?'

'Yep!' Durez said proudly. 'I just viewed the body of our latest shooting victim. Somebody you'd remember, Bart. The big yellow fellow who made the mistake of calling you Texas Jack!'

CHAPTER SIX

The news came as a shock to Bart.

'Somebody shot him?'

'Put a bullet neat through his head,' Doc said with a nod. 'Made a messy job of the back where it came out.' He paused. 'Funny thing. It looked like someone had beat him up as well. His right arm was broke like a dry twig.'

'Sounds like he had enemies,' Bart said dryly.

'Sheriff Hill is asking some questions around town right now,' Doc Webster said. 'I just hope none of the answers he gets gives him an idea you might be an interested party.'

Bart gave the old man an annoyed look. 'As far as I know, you were the only one who heard him speak to me.'

'There was quite a crowd around.'

'I don't think anyone else was interested enough to listen,' Bart snapped. 'And only those few words passed between us. Hardly enough to suggest I might have a reason for murdering him.'

Doc's purple face wore a knowing expression. 'It wouldn't look good to have your name mentioned in this case after just being cleared of Clancy Evans' murder. You know how folks put two and two together and enjoy coming up with the wrong answer.'

'Is that why you came all the way out here?'

The old man nodded. 'I wanted to be sure to warn you. I hadn't any idea where you might stand in the matter.' He took a short black pipe and a pouch of tobacco from a side coat pocket and began filling the pipe. 'Did you see him after you left the saloon, Bart?'

If Bart told him the truth, he knew not even Doc would believe he was innocent.

He said, 'I got my horse and came straight out here.'

Doc touched a match to his pipe and puffed a couple of times to get it going nicely before he spoke again. Then, removing it from his mouth for a moment, he said, 'I know you wouldn't shoot a man in cold blood, Bart.'

'Thank you,' he said sarcastically.

'I mean it,' Doc insisted. 'But someone did. And maybe that someone knew you and he had

had words and figured you might get blamed for any harm that came to him.'

'But we didn't have words,' Bart said with a touch of irritation. 'He made a drunken mistake, and I told him he was wrong.'

'So you did!' Doc agreed, puffing on the pipe.

Bart said, 'If the sheriff knows his job, he should be able to find out who among the big man's cronies did it. It's like as not one of the gang he rides with is guilty.'

'That's probably true, Bart,' Doc Webster said. 'But I wanted you to know all the facts.'

'Thanks,' Bart said, and left the barn to stride back toward the house. The doctor came trotting at his heels. At the rear door of the frame house, Bart turned and frowned at him.

'I expect you're going back to town,' he said. 'I have some things to do here this afternoon.'

Doc Webster looked startled. 'You mean I'm not welcome, Bart?'

'I mean I've got some private matters to attend to,' Bart said evenly, his lanky figure blocking the door.

The doctor shrugged. 'I'm not one to stay where I'm not wanted,' he said. 'I'll head back to Durez City and see what the latest developments are. You coming in town tonight, Bart?'

'I reckon so,' he said.

'I'll see you then,' Doc Webster promised. 'Same place?'

'I guess I'll be trying the Ace Saloon tonight,' Bart said slowly. 'I'll keep an eye open for you.'

'Do that,' Doc Webster urged. 'I may have some important news for you.'

He went back to the gray and mounted it with some difficulty. Then, with a genial wave to Bart, he rode off toward town. Bart watched to make sure he was well on his way before turning and entering the old house.

At dusk, he saddled up and rode off to keep his rendezvous.

In town, he decided to leave his horse at the livery stable for a couple of hours and picked the one next to the hotel and almost directly across from the Ace Saloon. A teen-aged lad took the bay and led it into the stable as Bart strolled back down the alley in the direction of the saloon.

It didn't appear to be as busy as on some of the other nights. He crossed the street, stepped up onto the wooden sidewalk and made his way through the swinging doors. There had been a few loiterers outside, but none of them seemed to recognize him or pay any attention to him. He was surprised to find no more than a half-dozen lined up at the long bar and maybe as many more sitting at a couple of the tables. There was no poker game going on; the big round table at which the late Clancy Evans had presided was deserted. Jim Malone couldn't have gotten another gambler to replace him yet.

Bart made his way to the bar and rested a spurred boot on the rail. He saw that a hired hand was tending the bar for Malone. The thin, unhappy-looking man approached him now and asked, 'What's yours, mister?'

'Double whiskey,' Bart said, ordering his usual.

The thin man returned with his drink, and he paid for it. Then he gulped down half the contents of the glass and helped himself to a chaser of water. After that he pulled out a small sack of tobacco and went about rolling himself a smoke. The warming effect of the whiskey relaxed him a little, and he listened to the drone of conversation going on around him and wondered if Doc Webster would show up.

Bart lit his cigarette and had another swallow of whiskey. He was about to down the last of it when he felt the touch of a hand on his elbow. He whirled around quickly, not knowing who it might be, and found himself staring into the fat, sardonic face of Jim Malone.

'You found your way back to the place again,' the fat man said with an unfriendly smile.

'There is not much choice in a town this size,' Bart said.

Jim Malone chuckled. It was obvious the saloon owner and town political boss was determined to maintain his pretense of being in a happy mood.

'Durez City is not such a bad town.'

'It could be all right,' Bart observed dryly. 'Just a few people want to hold it back.'

'I don't want you to think I hold anything against you on Clancy Evans' account,' Jim Malone said. 'In a way, he got what was coming to him. And anyhow, a jury said you weren't to blame.'

'Thanks,' Bart said.

The saloon owner sighed. 'A lot of people got wrong ideas about me.'

'I wouldn't know,' Bart said carefully.

'Yep. That's correct!' Jim Malone pulled out a cigar and, biting off the end, thrust it in his heavy-lipped mouth and touched a match to it.

He glanced at Bart's empty glass and waved to the unhappy-looking bartender. 'Give my friend another of whatever he had,' the owner ordered.

As the thin man hurried to refill Bart's glass with whiskey, Jim Malone smiled once more and said, 'This one is on the house.'

Bart regarded him coolly. 'I can't stop you throwing away your profits.'

The saloon owner chuckled at this. 'I like you, Landry,' he said. 'I don't see why you and me shouldn't get along.'

Bart picked up the filled glass. 'My price runs higher than a double whiskey,' he said before gulping it down.

Jim Malone glared at him and puffed furiously at the cigar for a moment. His fat face was wrathful as he pointed a stubby finger Bart's way and warned, 'I don't have to buy you with a double whiskey or anything else. You're the one in trouble here. You need me a lot worse than I'll ever need you.'

Bart continued to smile. 'Maggie warned me you were a charming man,' he said.

'Leave my daughter out of it!' Malone snapped.

'I think she'd like that.'

'I can handle her,' the saloon owner went on angrily. 'She comes to me meek enough when she needs money. All I have to do is wait.'

'You seem pretty worried for somebody so sure of the situation,' Bart commented.

'People in town here are beginning to ask what has happened to the Kingstons,' Jim Malone said.

Bart ignored the comment and instead studied the dregs in his glass. 'You know,' he drawled, 'This is pretty poor whiskey. You should bring in better stuff.'

Jim Malone's moon face went crimson. 'Don't give me advice on whiskey,' he snapped. 'I don't need it. You better be prepared to tell folks what you did to those two poor old people.'

Bart said, 'They're visiting in Santa Ana. They have a nephew there.'

'That's bunk!' Jim Malone told him. 'They never had a nephew in Santa Ana. The old woman had a younger brother there. And he's been dead a couple of years.'

This was news to Bart. He should have made sure who the relative in Santa Ana was. He shrugged. 'I might be wrong about who they're seeing. But that's where they headed. Maybe they have a son there.'

Jim Malone shook his head. 'Wrong again, Mister Landry!' he said sarcastically. 'The only son those two old people ever had was a boy who died back East before they came here. Mrs. Kingston decided she wanted to live in this part of the country because of her brother.'

Bart shrugged. 'Since you know all about them, why ask me?'

'Because I don't know the most important fact,' Jim Malone said. 'Where are they now?'

'Ask them when they get back.'

'I'm not asking them anything, nor you either,' Malone said angrily. 'But there is someone who does want to put a couple of questions to you. Sheriff Hill.'

'I don't see your partner around tonight,' Bart said, glancing about the nearly empty saloon. 'But you can tell him for me he can find me here whenever he wants to talk.'

'It happens that is right now,' Malone said with a sour smile. 'The sheriff is waiting out back in my office.' He put his half-smoked cigar back in his mouth and silently studied Bart.

'I'll talk to him,' Bart said. 'Lead the way.'

'It's a pleasure,' Jim Malone assured him, the smile returning to his fat face.

Bart followed him the length of the big main room. They went out through a plain door and down a long, dimly lighted corridor. Malone paused before a door far down on the left and swung it open. He waited for Bart to enter.

Sheriff Hill was seated behind the big desk that almost completely filled the tiny room. The square face of the elderly lawman was set in a grim look.

'So you found him, Jim,' he said in his gruff voice.

'Sure. We've been having a talk at the bar,' Malone agreed in his oily way. He came around to stand beside the sheriff where he could watch Bart's face.

The sheriff regarded Bart sternly. 'You've stirred up a heap of trouble in this town.'

'I can't agree with that,' Bart said quietly. 'The trouble was here.'

'I don't mean only with Clancy Evans,' Sheriff Hill told him, 'though the poor devil would probably still be alive if it weren't for you. But there are a lot of other things, like what's happened to the Kingstons.'

'Nothing. I've already told that to everyone more than once.'

'And nobody believes you!'

80

'I can't help that.'

The sheriff leaned forward. 'No one ever heard the Kingstons say they expected a visitor. No one ever heard them mention you. Yet one morning you're there and they're gone. On a vacation, you say! A vacation they began in the middle of the night!' The gruff voice reached a high point in sarcasm with the last few words.

Bart knew he could gain nothing by protesting his innocence. 'Is that all, Sheriff?' he asked.

'Not by a long shot!' The big man thumped his fist on the desk. 'We got some other questions, ain't we, Jim?'

Jim Malone, who had remained silent until now, nodded his bald head. 'A few our friend from out of town may have a hard time answering.'

'For one,' the sheriff said, 'how do we know your name is Bart Landry?'

Bart shrugged. 'Why should it be anything else?'

'That's another question,' the sheriff snapped. 'What I want to know now is if you have any proof about who you are.'

'I have no papers, if that's what you mean,' Bart said quietly.

Sheriff Hill exchanged a significant glance with Jim Malone. Bart could tell the interview was shaping up just the way they had hoped. A nasty smile crossed the burly face of the sheriff.

81

'So you have no papers or any identification at all,' he said. 'In other words, we don't know who you are!'

'If you want to take that attitude,' Bart said. 'In this country, a man's word usually counts unless there's a good reason to doubt it.'

'We've got reasons,' Sheriff Hill told him. 'Clancy Evans' murder, for one. And another murder last night of some outlaw who drifted into town. And maybe the two Kingstons to boot! We've got plenty of reasons!'

'A jury cleared me on Clancy Evans,' Bart said with great patience. 'I don't know anything about this other murder you've mentioned. And I certainly deny doing any harm to the Kingstons.'

The sheriff waved his arguments aside. 'Sure you deny everything. I know!' And then the hard eyes under the shaggy brows fixed on Bart as he asked, 'What do you know about Texas Jack?'

Bart went rigid at the mention of the familiar name again. He lost all his nonchalance as he tried to figure out just how much the sheriff and Jim Malone knew.

He asked, 'Who is Texas Jack?'

Sheriff Hill eyed the saloon owner, and they both broke into laughter. 'I sure have to hand it to you,' the burly man said. 'You got a good innocent line of talk.'

82

'I don't happen to know what you're talking about.'

Jim Malone gave him a triumphant look. 'You're telling us you never heard of Texas Jack?'

'I just asked who he is.'

Sheriff Hill became grim again. 'I know what you're trying to do, young fella,' he said. 'You're trying to dodge my questions. You know as well as Jim and me that Texas Jack is a train robber and killer. And it could be that you're him!'

Bart managed a laugh, but it wasn't too successful. 'What a compliment!'

'Not exactly,' the sheriff said. 'We've got information from the federal people that Texas Jack is headed this way. In fact, they think he may be making his headquarters somewheres not too far from here. And just as we get this word, you show up.'

Bart's pale blue eyes regarded the two calmly. He had regained control of himself and felt sure that once again he could outsmart them. 'That's easy figuring, Sheriff, just like two and two. Only trouble is that it's too easy! I don't happen to be Texas Jack. I'll bet if you match my description with his, you'll find I don't even look like him!'

The sheriff scowled. 'I don't have to tell you there ain't no description. No one on the side of the law has ever got a look at Texas Jack. All we know is he's tall and thin.'

83

'Just like Mister Landry here!' Jim Malone said with a significant expression on his fat face.

Bart regarded them coldly. 'If you two are through playing games, I'm going back to some serious drinking,' he said.

Sheriff Hill rose. 'Don't think we're finished with you,' he warned.

'I'll keep that in mind,' Bart said, his hand barely touching his .45.

'We'll have word from Santa Ana tomorrow,' the sheriff went on. 'And if the Kingstons ain't there, we'll expect you to do some talkin', and fast!'

'They won't be there,' Jim Malone assured him. 'He's lying. You can tell that.' As Bart turned and opened the door to go, the fat man shouted after him, 'And you keep away from my daughter! You hear that!'

Bart turned to offer a mocking grin. 'The problem may be to keep your daughter away from me!' And he left the two men standing by the desk glaring after him.

Back in the saloon, business had picked up. There was quite a crowd along the bar, and one of the new customers was Doc Webster. The old man saw Bart almost as soon as he came back into the big room and waved to him to come over.

The old man said, 'What's your pleasure, Bart?'

'The usual,' he said. 'I don't aim to stay here long.'

'Better change your plans,' Doc Webster warned him. And he ordered drinks for both of them.

Bart gave him a questioning glance. 'What is it now?'

'Nick Cressy!' Doc Webster said from the side of his mouth in a low tone. 'Don't let on, but he's outside waiting for you to leave.'

The pale blue eyes narrowed. 'That's interesting news.'

'He's out to pick a fight with you.'

Bart grinned. 'And I don't have to guess why. Maggie paid me a call at the Kingston place today after you left. One of his men followed her there.'

Doc Webster gave a low whistle. 'I can't think of a better way to get into trouble.'

The drinks came, and the old man paid for them. When the bartender left them, Doc Webster said, 'no matter what the reason, he's out there waiting. And if you're smart, you'll keep him waiting until he gets tired and leaves.'

'Why doesn't he come in here?'

'And take a chance on breaking up his future father-in-law's place? Jim wouldn't look kindly on that!'

Bart gave a grim smile. 'So I'm supposed to oblige by joining him outside. Maybe I will.' He took his drink.

Doc rubbed his grizzled chin. 'Nick is a

85

tough boy. And there are a lot of Diamond O cowpokes around to help if he starts losing to you. Most of them are renegades Jim has picked up in here, and all of them are gun-toting outlaws.'

'You make it sound like I'm in trouble.'

'Maybe you should stay away from town altogether.'

'Sorry. My business won't let me.'

Doc frowned at this. 'I wish you'd give me an idea just what your business is.'

Bart offered him a thin smile. 'I make old people like the Kingstons disappear. Better keep an eye on me.'

'That's the sheriff's line,' Doc said miserably. 'I don't go along with it.' He leaned close to Bart. 'Why don't you leave through the back?'

'And miss a chance to better my acquaintance with Nick?' he asked. 'That would be a pity.'

Doc sighed. 'Well, if you've decided on trouble, I'll stand by to do any free doctoring. That's all I can promise.'

Bart laughed and clapped a hand on the old man's shoulder. 'One thing about you, Doc. You always face up to the worst.'

'There isn't any best to this situation,' the old man said glumly, ready to leave the bar and follow Bart.

When Bart pushed open the swinging doors and stepped down onto the wooden sidewalk, he saw that a crowd had gathered for the expected battle between him and Nick Cressy. Nick must have spread the word around he was out to get Bart, or his men had. It amounted to the same thing. Bart found himself standing in the middle of a ring of unfriendly faces. And stationed at the outer edge of the sidewalk directly opposite him was the dandified Nick Cressy.

'You kept me waiting quite a time, Landry,' Nick said with a nasty smile.

'I only just found out you were here,' Bart said quietly. 'Doc told me.' He nodded toward the old man, who was standing at his side and slightly behind him.

'Now that you're here, what's it to be—guns or fists?' Nick asked with swaggering bravado. He was clearly playing to the assembled crowd.

Bart gave him a derisive smile. 'I'm not sure you're man enough to handle either.'

Nick took an angry step toward him. 'You talk big! But then you just murdered two sixty-year-olds! That makes him a real killer, eh, boys?' This sally was greeted by loud laughter from his backers.

Doc Webster glanced nervously at the circle of onlookers and tugged Bart's arm. 'It's not too late to back down and leave,' he whispered urgently. 'You don't stand a chance with this bunch!'

Bart paid no attention to him; the pale blue

87

eyes were fixed on Nick. 'If tongues were the weapons, you'd probably do first rate, Nick. But I aim to cut you up with my fists, to make you pretty for Maggie!' And he unbuckled his gun belt and gave it to Doc Webster.

His last remark had the effect he hoped on the young foreman of the Diamond O. Nick's thin, handsome face showed pure rage as he fumbled in a rapid attempt to rid himself of his holster. When at last he had it off, he crouched and clenched his fists in readiness for Bart. The circle of the crowd widened, and a hush came over the noisy group as the two men prepared to battle in the dim light issuing through the saloon entrance.

Bart moved in on his opponent. And then Nick hit him with brutal force, lifting every ounce of power from his lithe body into the surprise uppercut. It sent Bart reeling back. Doc had warned him the foreman would be nasty, and this was proof of it!

A savage elation showed in Nick's wild young face as he came forward quickly to build on this fast start. But he was too eager and too fast. His next blow skidded across Bart's shoulder, and the impetus carried Nick on past him. Bart grabbed Nick's arm and whirled him violently. Then he belted him flush on the jaw. It was a short, crisp, immaculate blow. Nick's mouth jarred open and his eyes glazed as he stumbled. Then Bart clouted him just once again, on the right cheek. The flesh split like the skin of a burst peach, and blood gushed out. Bart stepped back and deliberately waited for the battered Nick to fall. He did.

There was hushed silence from the onlookers.

Bart turned to the astonished Doc Webster retrieved his gun belt and buckled it on. Then he said, 'Let's get away from here!' and impatiently shoved his way through the crowd.

CHAPTER SEVEN

Bart headed straight across the street to the alley that led to the livery stable. Doc hurried along at his side, having to make an effort to keep up with the tall man's giant, angry strides. The old man didn't say anything until they had left the crowd well behind.

Then the purple face looked up at Bart with admiration. 'I haven't seen fighting like that in some time,' he said. 'You've got style, mister.'

'I wanted to end it fast,' Bart said, his bony face grim. And he strode along, staring straight ahead.

'That's the way you handled it.' Doc Webster chortled with laughter. 'You sure did make Nick pretty for Maggie just the way you promised.'

'I hope that ends it.'

'Don't count on that,' Doc warned.

They came to the door of the livery stable, and Bart signaled to the youth in charge that he wanted his horse and then turned to Doc while he waited for the bay to be brought out.

'I'm going back to the house,' he said.

'Keep a sharp eye out,' Doc Webster cautioned him. 'Some of the Diamond O crowd may decide to give you trouble.'

'I doubt that.'

'It's more liable to happen than not,' Doc said. 'Nick isn't above getting them to go after you.'

The boy came out with the bay saddled and ready to go. Bart paid him and swung up into the saddle. He gave Doc Webster one of his grim smiles.

'There wasn't much need of free doctoring for me, after all.'

The old man hung onto the side of his saddle and looked up at him with worried eyes. 'Don't cheer too soon,' he said.

'Nothing more to tell me?'

'Not much,' Doc Webster said, licking his purple lips nervously. 'Only some people around town think that fellow that was shot last night was Texas Jack.' The old man paused. 'Of course I know that isn't so. I heard him mistake you for that outlaw in the saloon.'

'Better forget what you heard,' Bart said crisply.

Doc raised his eyebrows. 'If that's what you want, Bart.'

'It could save a lot of pain all around.'

'Sure, Bart! You know they tell me that Texas Jack is a great man with his fists, just like you!'

Bart's eyes narrowed. 'I'm getting out of here,' he said. 'The longer I stay, the more ideas that crowd may get.'

'Good luck, Bart!' the old man said, letting go of the saddle. 'And be careful!'

He rode down the alley with the Doc's warning in his ears. A strange old man! In the street, he saw the crowd in front of the saloon had melted away. He rode past the entrance without catching a glimpse of Nicky Cressy or his henchmen.

The bay jogged along at a good pace, with Bart absorbed in his thoughts. Soon Durez City was behind him and half the distance to the Kingston place had been covered. He shivered, for the night, which had been merely cool before, was downright cold now. And it was silent as well, so silent it bothered Bart.

He took the makings from his shirt pocket, rolled himself a smoke and lit it without halting the bay's easy progress. The flare of the match in the dark illuminated his hard-set face, then winked out as he took a deep drag on the cigarette. There were just the stars and the dark outlines of the hills in the distance. All the long length of the road he met no one. Then just ahead there loomed the outline of the Kingston place. He headed the bay off the road and toward the stable.

Suddenly the horse whinnied nervously and hesitated. In that second Bart sensed danger. He peered ahead into the darkness but could see nothing. Then, from somewhere to the right, there was a flash of orange and he felt a burning sensation along the ridge of his scalp. At once faintness overcame him. He slipped from the saddle, knowing he'd been hit, and as he fell on the ground he heard the sound of horses' hooves bearing down on him and the shouting, jubilant voices of many riders.

His mind was still reeling as he fumbled for the .45 and fired blindly at his attackers. There was another orange flash close at hand, and a bullet bit the ground near him. Then he felt the fierce, pawing impact of a horse's shod hoof on his leg and barely moved it in time to save himself from the full weight of the maddened beast. All was confusion, noise and danger!

And then when it seemed he was about to die at the mercy of these unknown adversaries, he heard new shots from a short distance away. The milling riders who had closed in on him quickly broke rank, and there were hoarse oaths, frightened shouting and more bullets fired as they began to ride off. One gave a loud cry and plunged from his mount to lie near Bart on the ground.

It was as if a miracle had happened. Within a matter of seconds Bart was left alone again with only the motionless form of the attacker who had been shot down stretched out a few feet away to keep him company. He raised himself on an elbow and stared up into the darkness to try and see who his rescuer had been. And in a moment he saw a tall figure coming near with cautious steps.

'Are you all right, Mr. Landry?' The precise voice was familiar.

'Yes,' he managed weakly. 'I got hit, but nothing serious.' He made a great effort and struggled to his feet, his head still reeling.

The tall man came forward quickly and grasped him by the arm. 'My dear sir, you're swaying on your feet!' And now Bart knew the voice. It was none other than Mayor Peters, Durez City's eccentric undertaker and politician.

'I'm lucky you came along,' he gasped. 'The second time I owe you my life.'

The mayor seemed alarmed. 'I'm not sure whether it's saved or ebbing away. Hadn't we better go inside and see how badly you're hurt?'

Bart touched a hand to his head. 'Yes. That would be best.' He nodded toward the other man on the ground, who had made no move. 'What about him?'

The mayor glanced around at the still form.

'One of your attackers, Mr. Landry. But I suppose there is such a thing as Christian charity!' And he left Bart for a moment to go over to him. He bent over the fallen man briefly, then got up and came back. 'He is quite dead, Mr. Landry. I fear he will require nothing more of me than my professional services.' And taking Bart's arm again, he helped him the short remaining distance to the house.

The mayor bathed his wound by the kitchen lamp and sputtered about the hazards of travel with such ruffians abroad. 'You are lucky, Mr. Landry,' he said, as he used a section of an old pillow case to bandage his head. 'Just a little deeper, and it wouldn't have mattered whether I arrived when I did or not.'

Bart's head was clearer now, and he was beginning to put the pieces of the puzzle together. 'They jumped me when I rode into the yard,' he said. 'I think they were some of the Diamond O crowd. I had a row with Nick Cressy in town tonight.'

Mayor Peters' bloodhound face regarded him sadly. 'Violence, young man,' he said, 'seems to be your constant companion. Surely you must realize that it will bring you to me or one of my associates in the end.'

Bart was forced to smile. 'It nearly did tonight. You lost me as a customer when you came to my rescue.'

'I fear I do have a substitute, though,' the mayor said, nodding toward where the dead man lay outside. 'And it is produced by my own hand.' He sighed. 'I think this is going to be somewhat awkward to explain.'

'I'll back you up,' Bart promised. 'I'll let them know you did it to save my life; not just to sell a casket and embalming job.'

'You must remember your word doesn't stand for much in Durez City just now,' the mayor reminded him. 'I prefer to stand on my own dignity. Surely they will not dare question their mayor.'

'Whatever way you like,' Bart said. 'Will you take the body back as well?'

'I have my carriage with me, and there just happen to be two coffins in it. I was coming from providing one for a miner who died up in the hills. His partners wouldn't leave their stake to bring him to the city and sent a message for me to come up and attend to him and bring a suitable casket.'

'You believe in providing service,' Bart said.

'No trouble is too great for the dear departed,' Mayor Peters said with a deep sigh. 'They selected the best of the three, a carved mahogany with silver handles. It took longer than I expected, and I found myself heading for town at this late hour.'

'Lucky for me.'

He regarded Bart with upraised eyebrows.

95

'Perhaps it was a stroke of fate. At any rate, it is very convenient. I will be able to take this poor fellow back in the very casket he'll be buried in. I'm sure either Nick Cressy or the town will look after his funeral expenses.'

Bart stood up, still feeling rather shaky. 'I'll help you with him,' he said. 'And I've still got to bed down my bay.'

'Are you sure you feel up to that much exertion?' Mayor Peters asked anxiously.

'I'll be all right now,' Bart assured him. 'And I don't see them coming back, though you'd think they'd want to do something for the fellow you shot.'

The mayor shook his head. 'They are basically renegades and cowards. We gave them a bad scare, and they'll be quick to run for cover.'

'If this is one of the Cressy crowd, I should prefer charges against them with the sheriff,' Bart said.

The doleful man showed surprise. 'You are naïve enough to think that would do any good?'

Bart sighed. 'I suppose not.'

'Be content that you are safe, my boy,' the mayor said. 'And better be more careful in future.'

'I will,' he promised. And then, staring at the eccentric man with the professionally sad air and somber clothes: 'I must say you're an

96

excellent shot. You handled your gun like a veteran.'

'Most people in this country require a knowledge of weapons,' he said with a sigh. He put on his dark stovepipe hat. 'I will tell Doc Webster to come out and look at that head of yours in the morning.'

Bart touched the bandage. 'I want to get rid of this as soon as I can.'

'Better not hurry,' the mayor advised him. 'You have a nasty flesh wound there. And now I suppose we must proceed to our unhappy duty.'

Bart went out into the cold darkness, and together they carried the body of the dead gunman to the wagon. The mayor removed the lid from one of the two coffins, and they slid the body in it. Bart felt a chill go through him as the mayor closed the lid down again. He knew it was only good fortune that he wasn't a limp body in a casket as well. He stood by while the mayor got up on the seat of the wagon and drove off, with the dead man's horse following, its reins tied to the rear of the wagon. It made a strange sight. In a moment they were lost in the night, although Bart stood and listened to the sounds of the wagon and horses' hooves long after they were out of sight. At last he turned and found the bay, took it into the stable and unsaddled it and looked after it for the night.

The injury to his head and the weird turn of events had left him in a weary, confused state. He decided to stretch out on the cot just as he

97

was. And for the first time he left the lamp burning. In the back of his mind was the idea the riders might return before dawn, and he didn't want to be caught completely unprepared. He took his .45 from the holster and placed it beside him so he could handily lift it. Then, resigned to the fact he'd taken all possible precautions, he tried to sleep.

He came awake suddenly with a splitting headache and was aware of a loud pounding on the kitchen door. Confused and not fully realizing what time it was, he reached for the .45 and rose with it in his hand. Then he saw that morning had come. He stood a moment in the center of the kitchen. The knocking on the door was repeated even more loudly.

'Jehoshaphat, Bart!' Doc Webster called out plaintively on the other side of the locked door. 'You must really be dead!'

So that was who it was! A tired smile crossed Bart's face.

Still feeling giddy, he went over to the door and unbolted it. Doc Webster thrust his mottled face in, wearing an almost comical expression of worry. 'I danged near burst a blood vessel waiting for you to open up,' he exclaimed, full of indignation. 'From what Mayor Peters told me, you got a bad wound. I thought it might have been worse than he knew.'

Bart couldn't help feeling gratitude for Doc's

concern. He said, 'I'm good for another round or two with Nick Cressy yet.'

The doctor gave him a scornful glance with his bloodshot eyes. 'Not right now you're not,' he said. And placing his battered doctor's bag on the table, he pulled out a chair for Bart to sit down on. 'Come over here and let me take a look at that head.' He was all the medical man this morning, in spite of shaky hands and a fragrant brandy breath.

Bart sat in the chair. 'The mayor cleaned it up and put on that bandage for me,' he said. 'In fact, I was lucky he came along, or the Cressy bunch would have finished me. The mayor is a crack shot.'

'He may be handy with a rifle but he doesn't know much about a bandage,' the old doctor grumbled as he worked on Bart's head. 'He's got you bound up like a Christmas package. You don't need all that.' He removed the old bandage and applied something to the wound he assured Bart would do wonders but which made him wince. The doctor worked on as he kept up a running conversation and finally put on a much smaller gauze bandage than the mayor's makeshift one.

He closed his bag. 'That will do until tomorrow,' he said. 'Have to keep the dressings changed pretty regular until that heals.'

Bart grimaced and touched a hand to his head

so he could feel the bandage. 'This was the last thing I needed.'

Doc Webster studied him grimly. 'I told you to be careful. You think I'm just a crazy old drunk. But I knew enough about Nick Cressy and his hoodlums to guess what they'd try next.'

Bart rose. 'Want some breakfast?' he asked.

'I could use some strong coffee,' Doc Webster said, seating himself heavily in the chair Bart had just vacated. 'It's a long ride from Durez City on an empty stomach.' He gave him a sharp glance. 'Be a lot more sensible if you would let me bunk here with you until that head is better.'

Bart's reply was a curt, 'No!'

Doc sighed and shook his head. 'I don't understand you, son,' he said. 'I'd be willing to bet my last dollar you were straight as they come if it wasn't for this business here.'

Bart kept busy at the stove, with his back to the old man. 'Things might be a lot simpler if you didn't try so hard to figure them out,' he advised.

'Maybe,' Doc Webster said. 'But there is something you're trying to hide. It has to do with the Kingstons and this place. And it worries me that it might not be pretty.'

Bart moved back to the table and began setting out their places. He shot the old man a cynical look. 'Thanks for your confidence. Why

100

not tag me a murderer, same as the rest of Durez City?'

'No,' Doc said slowly. 'It wouldn't be as simple as that. If you've done anything to those old folks, there has to be a reason; something so big or black you felt you had to do what you did.' He paused. 'I hope you'll be able to make other folks see it that way when the time comes.'

Bart made no answer to this, and the old man became silent and moody, which was somewhat unusual for him. They sat down to breakfast, and it wasn't until they had finished and Bart was enjoying a cigarette and the Doc his short black pipe that the old man chuckled aloud as a sign he had regained his good humor.

'I'd sure like to have seen the mayor light into those fellows,' he said. 'I didn't think old embalming fluid had it in him.'

Bart exhaled two thin spirals of smoke and smiled. 'He lost no time. There wasn't any to lose. If one of them hadn't drilled me, their horses would have gotten me. I have a bad bruise on my leg as it is.'

'He was up in the hills, so he says,' Doc said, 'looking after a miner. He goes out that way once in a while.'

'So I gathered,' Bart said. 'He really seems to take a deep interest in his undertaking. Wonder he ever accepted the job of mayor.'

'They had a hard time persuading him,' Doc said, touching a match to his pipe, which had

101

gone out. 'I think he took it mainly because he hates the sheriff so much.'

'I didn't know that.'

Doc nodded. 'Him and the sheriff have feuded ever since the sheriff took over. In the old days, the sheriff used to have the undertaker from Deer Ridge come and look after any bodies that came his way. Soon as Mayor Peters took office, there was a new ruling. All the burying was to be done right in Durez City, with him officiating and the town paying the costs.'

Bart smiled. 'I'm beginning to get the picture.'

'So you've got the sheriff and Jim Malone lined up on one side and Mayor Peters and the fairly honest voters on the other,' Doc said, puffing contentedly on his short pipe. 'And the mayor still takes off for Chicago or St. Louis every now and then and spends a week or two ordering a new lot of fancy coffins. I'd say he has enough coffins in stock to bury all of Durez City, with a few left over to look after anybody who came down from the hills.'

'Lucky for me he wasn't away on one of his buying trips last night.'

'You can be sure of that,' Doc commented, giving him a sharp look. 'And don't think it's going to be any safer tonight or any night from now on. Nick Cressy won't rest until he gets even with you for peeling off his skin-deep

102

beauty in front of a good part of the town. You cut him up right smart!'

'I thought that might end it,' Bart said.

'Wait until Maggie sees him and hears about what happened,' Doc said. 'Don't think she won't make the most of it.'

'It was Maggie coming here who began the trouble.'

'Maggie likes trouble same as I like brandy,' Doc said. 'It's a kind of disease with her.'

Before Bart had a chance to make any comment on this, there was the sound of riders coming into the yard. Bart got up quickly, went to the window and pulled back the curtain in time to see Sheriff Hill and his deputy dismount.

He gave the old man a knowing look. 'The law has arrived,' he said and, without waiting for the sheriff's knock, went to the door to meet him.

Sheriff Hill paused a few steps from the door. The square face was grim. 'I thought you might have high-tailed it out of here,' he said.

Bart went outside to face him and the deputy who stood in the background. 'What gave you that idea?'

The sheriff's lip curled slightly. 'Things must be getting pretty hot, even for you.' His hard, small eyes fixed on Bart's bandaged head. 'You got a souvenir from last night.'

'Nothing that will slow me down,' he said.

Doc Webster came out of the house and stood beside Bart. Doc grinned and said, 'Good to know the law is taking an interest in the crime situation in Durez City. That Cressy bunch should be run out of town by rights. You should make the Diamond O get a full new crew.'

'Better be careful what you say, Doctor,' the sheriff said with a sarcastic emphasis on the 'doctor.' 'Just because a cowpoke who happened to work for the Diamond O outfit once gets plugged don't mean he was riding with Diamond O boys when it happened.'

Doc Webster's mottled face showed derision. 'So that's going to be the alibi. Funny it happened so soon after Bart beat the stuffing out of Nick.'

'I missed that,' Sheriff Hill said dourly. And, turning his attention to Bart: 'You keep on making trouble the way you've done since you come here, and you'll wind up in one of the mayor's wooden overcoats.'

'Is that what you came all the way out here to tell me?' Bart asked.

The sheriff shook his head. 'No. We came to ask a few questions about last night.'

'Ask as many as you want.'

'All we've got is the mayor's version of things,' the square-faced man said grimly. 'We want a few more facts.'

'When I rode into the yard, some of Nick's

men jumped me,' Bart said. 'If the mayor hadn't shown up, they'd have finished me.'

'Of course that's a guess on your part,' Sheriff Hill drawled. He gave Bart a sullen look. 'Me and my man will just take a look around.'

Bart nodded. But he could feel his nerves go tense again as the two lawmen began to search minutely the ground of the yard. He had an impulse to glance over in the direction of the barn and make sure the camouflage of scattered lumber still concealed the newly turned earth. But he knew he mustn't. So he forced himself to look the other way, toward the road where they were making their inspection now.

Doc Webster said, 'Those two would like nothing better than more trouble.'

'They might have cooked some up for me if you hadn't been here.'

The old man chuckled. 'I've been trying to prove how useful I could be. But you won't listen.'

Bart didn't answer, for his attention had been caught by something happening in the area of the yard where the main action of the melée had taken place the night before. Sheriff Hill had suddenly bent down and picked something from the ground, and now he and his deputy were discussing it, apparently with no little excitement.

Bart's pale blue eyes narrowed. 'Something's

doing,' he said, and started over toward the two lawmen.

'Don't get on your high horse,' Doc begged as he followed. 'Take it easy, no matter what. Remember the sheriff has the law behind that six-shooter he totes.'

Sheriff Hill turned as they approached, a strange smile on his square face. 'You gents look a mite worried,' he said, concealing his discovery in his half-closed right hand.

'Just interested,' Bart said.

'You ought to be,' the sheriff said, opening his hand for Bart and Doc Webster to see. In his palm was a large Mexican gold coin with a bullet hole drilled neatly through it. 'Ever seen anything like that before?' the sheriff asked.

Bart shook his head. 'No.'

Sheriff Hill chuckled and stuffed the gold piece in his pocket. 'Didn't think you'd say yes,' he observed dryly. 'There's a special story behind that drilled piece. It's a kind of calling card. I don't s'pose you'd ever admit hearing about it. But the story goes that Texas Jack leaves one of those pieces every time he kills a man. Sort of like laughin' at the law!'

CHAPTER EIGHT

Bart shrugged and said nothing. Secretly he was glad the sheriff had come upon the drilled gold piece. At least it took his attention away from other things, especially that spot near the barn with its tell tale fresh earth. But it wasn't good that the sheriff connected the Mexican piece with Texas Jack.

Doc Webster was the first to speak. He said, 'What kind of a crazy yarn is that! I've seen hundreds of gold dollars drilled with a bullet in my time. A lot of would-be badmen rig them up and carry them to give the idea they're crack shots.'

'But they're not like this one,' the sheriff said with an unpleasant smile. 'This one is special.'

'What's so special about it?' the old doctor demanded.

'It's identical with the ones Texas Jack always leaves,' the Sheriff said. 'Can you explain that, Mr. Landry?'

Bart eyed the square-faced man coolly. 'Likely it fell out of the pocket of the hombre Mayor Peters drilled.'

'Or maybe it fell out of yours, Mr. Landry,' the sheriff snapped. 'Or you could have left it there, if you were Texas Jack.'

'Which I don't happen to be!'

'You've got no papers to prove it!'

Bart said, 'What do you have to prove that I am?'

'I've got this gold piece,' the sheriff said. 'And sometime today we'll have word from Santa Ana. If the Kingstons didn't go there, you're going to have to come into the Durez City jail and do some explaining.'

Doc Webster scoffed. 'You're making a lot out of nothing, Sheriff. Bart is right. That gold piece likely fell out of the dead man's pocket.'

'And there were plenty of others here last night,' Bart reminded the sheriff. 'I suggest you try questioning some of Nick Cressy's men.'

Sheriff Hill scowled. 'I'll run my office the way I see fit,' he said. 'Don't be surprised if we pay another call on you later in the day.'

The sheriff and his deputy went back to their horses and rode off in the direction of Durez City. In spite of what had happened, Bart watched them go with a sense of relief. It could have been worse.

Doc glanced at him. 'How did you like that?'

'I'd say they'll keep trying until they have some sort of case trumped up against me. He mightn't have found that gold piece here at all. He could have brought it with him and pretended to find it.'

Doc Webster's purple face took on a stunned look. 'By thunder, you're right, Bart. He could have done just that.'

'One way or another, he wants to make out I'm Texas Jack.'

The old man frowned. 'He's been talking that story up around town. Now he must figure he's safe in bringing it out into the open.' He eyed Bart closely. 'You aren't hiding something from me, are you, son?'

'What do you mean?'

'The sheriff appears mighty certain you're tied up with Texas Jack in some way. And then that fellow the other night, the one who was murdered—he called you Texas Jack.'

'He soon back-tracked when I told him he was wrong,' Bart pointed out.

'Could be he was frightened.'

'Of me?'

'I say it could be.'

Bart frowned at the doctor. 'In that case, you think I may be Texas Jack?'

'I don't know what to think any more,' the old man worried.

'Then take the advice I've tried to give you. Don't think about it at all.' Bart paused and sighed. 'My head is pounding again.'

'Too much excitement,' the doctor said. 'You better go into the house and try to rest awhile. I'll give you something to make you sleep.'

'Hardly safe for me to close my eyes any more,' Bart complained as they headed toward the kitchen door.

Doc went to his battered bag that was still

109

resting on the kitchen table and brought out a small bottle of yellow liquid. He handed it to Bart.

'Take a tablespoonful of that whenever you need to sleep,' he told him. 'It will help.'

'Maybe if I could just get an hour or so alone—' Bart said with meaning.

The old man took the hint. He put on his hat and picked up his bag. 'You better keep away from Durez City tonight. Unless I see you before, I'll come back tomorrow morning.'

'I'll be all right,' Bart said wearily.

'Maybe.' Doc sounded doubtful. He hesitated a moment as if to add something more, then seemingly changed his mind. He turned and went on out.

Bart put the bottle of yellow medicine aside, went over to the cot and stretched out on it.

He had no idea how long he slept, but when he woke up his first reaction was that an angel was watching him. But when his sleep-fogged eyes cleared he saw it was no angel but Maggie Malone, looking pertly attractive in a fancy fawn riding habit, who smiled down at him.

He quickly raised himself on an elbow. 'How long have you been here?' he demanded.

She touched a surprisingly dainty hand to his chest. 'Relax,' she said. 'I've been here almost a half-hour. I've been watching you sleep. It made me feel deliciously wifely.'

Bart was forced to smile. 'There's nothing

110

delicious about my snoring.'

'You were very quiet.' Her blue eyes studied his bandaged head. 'Is that wound bad?'

'Just a scratch.'

'I'm sorry.'

'About what?'

Maggie lifted an eyebrow. 'Because I'm to blame, of course. If Nick's man hadn't seen me come here and told him, this would never have happened.'

'They've been after me anyway,' he said.

'Nick told me yesterday afternoon he was going to lay for you last night.'

He frowned. 'You saw him after you left here?'

'At the ranch. He promised to settle with you real fancy. Instead, you were the one who put him in his place. I could kiss you for that!'

He sat up on the cot beside her. 'I've decided you're a dangerous young woman,' he announced. 'Too dangerous for me.'

Maggie gave him a roguish smile. 'That doesn't sound like Texas Jack.'

Bart jumped up with a groan. 'Not you, too!'

'Everyone in Durez City says you're Texas Jack.'

'Not everyone,' Bart said, glancing down sternly at her pretty face. 'Maybe your father, Sheriff Hill and that crowd. They are the ones starting the rumor.'

'I hope it's true.'

'You must be out of your mind!'

She shook her head, the blue eyes eager with excitement. 'I have it all planned. You can rob the town bank. I know when Dad will be making his big deposit of the month, and then we'll run away together.'

Bart studied her smiling face in wonder. 'You think you'd enjoy being a bank robber's girl?'

'Wife,' she corrected him. 'We'd be married.'

'I doubt if we could stop long enough to have a judge say the words,' Bart said.

'I'd be willing to wait until it was safe,' she assured him.

'Very generous of you.' He bowed. 'You must cotton to the idea of living in outlaw hideouts, being shut off from decent people, never knowing when a sheriff's bullet is going to cut down the person you love.'

Maggie continued to smile. 'It sounds exciting!'

'It isn't really,' he said with a weary expression. 'Before long you'd wish you were safely back in Durez City.'

'Dad is as crooked as they come, and he has always prospered,' she said. 'I don't see why you make the life sound so bad.'

'Your father has managed to keep his crookedness on the right side of the law so far,' Bart reminded her. 'That makes a lot of difference.'

'Dad is the law in Durez City,' she said

112

scornfully. 'You couldn't count Sheriff Hill. He does whatever Dad tells him.'

'And the fact that both your father and Nick Cressy think you are sweet on me makes it just that much worse,' Bart complained. 'Are you anxious to get me shot or strung up?'

'Neither one,' she said. 'You know I'm in love with you.'

'That's only because you want me to rob a bank for you,' he said bitterly.

'No, I mean it, Bart,' she said. 'I do like you.'

He spread his hands. 'Then prove it. Get away from here. Forget me. Forget I ever lived. Don't keep your father and Nick after me.'

'They won't dare do much,' she said airily. 'You have Mayor Peters on your side.'

He gave a grim sigh. 'I don't think I should count on him. If they offered him the price of an especially fancy funeral for me, he might swing over to them.'

'No, he wouldn't,' Maggie said. 'He saved your life last night.'

'That was a lucky accident.'

'And you should see Nick's face,' Maggie exclaimed jubilantly. 'It's all swollen and out of shape. I met him in the yard of the ranch, and when he saw me he turned and went the other way. But I had a good look at him.'

'You're a regular little savage,' Bart said with

113

wonderment. 'Doc was right. You really do enjoy trouble.'

Maggie got up and came close to him. 'I don't care who you are,' she said, 'or even what you've done. Maybe you are Texas Jack, and you've killed the Kingstons and a lot of other people, but I'm in love with you and want you to take me away from here.'

Bart took her firmly by the arms and held her away from him, looking into her eyes with a grave expression. 'You're pretty exciting yourself. But I've had more than my share of excitement. I want you to be sensible. Go back to town and don't ever come out here again.'

'I won't promise,' she warned him. 'You can't make me.'

He sighed. 'No. I don't suppose I can.'

The roguish blue eyes met his appealingly. 'Tell me the truth about yourself, Bart—the real truth! I won't let on to anyone. I just have to know!'

His own eyes became hard. 'Are you sure your father didn't send you out to soften me up and get that information from me?'

He still had her arms firmly in his grasp, and her eyes suddenly took on a frightened expression. She answered in an incredulous tone, 'You don't really think that?'

'You're just a little too curious about me,' he said.

'For myself! Not for Dad or anyone else!'

'I know that's what you want me to believe,'

he said. 'But is it the truth?'

Hurt tears brimmed over the lids of the roguish blue eyes, and Bart felt her small, lithe body suddenly become limp. 'You know I wouldn't double-cross you, Bart. I like you too much. And I have no one, no one at all!'

He was suddenly sorry for the lovely blonde girl. He let her go and stared down at the worn linoleum of the Kingstons' kitchen floor. 'I'm sorry, Maggie,' he said. 'I've been on the run so long it's not hard for me to become suspicious of the wrong people.'

'It's all right,' she answered in a low voice. 'It's only I thought you would understand.'

'I do,' he said. 'Believe me, I do.' He raised his eyes to stare at the pretty face, all its pertness vanished now. 'I'm trying to protect you, not only from me but from yourself.'

Some of her old bravado returned. 'Pretty speeches!' she said.

'I mean what I'm saying,' he insisted. And he was about to explain when he looked up and saw someone else standing just inside the kitchen door.

'I didn't intend to intrude,' Eve Driscoll said in her modulated Eastern voice. She was dressed in an expensive white dress with dark trimming at the neck and down the front.

Bart found his voice. 'You're not intruding. I'm glad to see you.'

Eve turned. 'Since you have company, I had better go.'

Now it was Maggie Malone who spoke up loudly. 'You don't have to leave on my account, Miss Driscoll,' she said. 'I'm on my way.' She turned to Bart with a bitter smile. 'I didn't know you were expecting your girl friend. No wonder you kept asking me to leave!' And with another smile and a nod for Eve as she passed on the way out, Maggie left.

Bart sighed. 'You mustn't take her too seriously. She's upset.'

Eve Driscoll was unsmiling. 'Obviously,' she said.

'Where did you come from?' he asked.

'I've been in Durez City,' she said. 'Father had one of the boys drive me in the carriage so I could do some shopping.'

That explained why she was all dressed up. Bart began to get over the first shock of embarrassment. He waved toward a chair. 'Won't you sit down?' he asked. 'The place is pretty much of a mess, but I had an accident last night.'

'I heard about it,' she said in the same calm, expressionless tone. 'I also heard about your brawl with Nick Cressy.'

'If you'd let me explain—' he said.

'I'm afraid I haven't time for that,' she said. 'I don't want to keep the carriage waiting. But I heard something in Durez City I thought you should know.'

116

Bart knew she was angry and felt he couldn't blame her. No doubt she had rushed out hoping to help him and had discovered him with another girl.

He said, 'Look; I'm sorry about everything.' He pushed forward a plain kitchen chair. 'Won't you sit for just a minute?'

She shook her head. 'Thank you, no. I only wanted to tell you that Jim Malone has had word from Santa Ana. The Kingstons are not there.'

'Oh?' he said.

Her brown eyes fixed on him scornfully. 'But then that isn't news to you, I suppose. You've known that all the time.'

He shrugged. 'You wouldn't believe me if I said no.'

'I wouldn't.' She was emphatic.

'I don't think you should worry too much about it,' he said, at the end of a short silence between them.

Eve Driscoll, elegant in her smart town clothes, looked around the shabby kitchen and, with something close to horror and disgust in her voice, said, 'This was home for those poor old people. What did you do to them, Mr. Landry?'

So it was back to Mr. Landry again, he thought wearily. Eve's visit couldn't have been worse timed. He found himself groping for the proper words.

117

'Just let all this rest for a few days,' he urged her at last. 'Don't try to make a quick judgment. I promise I'll explain to you when I can.'

She shook her head. 'You'll have gone by then. They say you're Texas Jack, that you killed the Kingstons because you thought they had gold hidden here.'

His cheek twitched in an involuntary nervous tic. 'Do you think I did that?'

'I don't know what to believe,' she said.

'You didn't feel that way the other day,' he reminded her.

'I didn't know what I do now,' she said. 'You'll have to answer to the law for what's happened here.'

'Why do you think I've stayed on in this place?'

She shrugged. 'Perhaps you think you can brazen it out. But there is some law left here. My father will see you are properly punished!'

And with that she turned and went out the back door.

Losing no time, he went out to the stable and saddled the bay. It was nearing five o'clock when he started out. He decided against using the road and instead made his way along a back trail that also led to the outskirts of Durez City. The barren country had an unfriendly air, and after about twenty minutes he began to wonder if he had lost his way. He saw ahead of him a

118

grassy swale that ran on a few yards, then dipped and narrowed into a sandy draw clogged with brush. To his left, the terrain was uneven and rocky, undulating away into a gray wasteland. Some hundred yards to his right there was a wooded ridge that cast a shadow on the flank of a hill dotted with yellow snakeweed. The trail seemed to lead to the ridge and by it. He jogged the bay and rode on, anxious to get into town.

Reaching Durez City, he avoided the main streets and made his way to Mayor Peters' undertaking establishment by a circuitous route. He didn't leave the bay tied to the hitching post, but rode down an alley behind the gray building and tethered the bay to a tree out back. Then, making sure there was no one around, he dodged furtively into the office entrance.

The wizened clerk was at his usual post behind the big desk.

'Yes?' he inquired in his rasping voice.

'Mayor Peters,' Bart said. 'I need to see him right away.'

'He isn't here,' the sickly old man snapped.

'Where can I reach him?'

'You can't,' the clerk said. 'He left on the stage for St. Louis today.'

This was a shocking blow to Bart's hopes. He'd counted on the mayor for his main support, and now he was gone. And there

119

wasn't a chance he would be back in time to do any good.

He said, 'Thanks,' and turned toward the door.

'If it's about a funeral, I can fix you up,' the wizened man said, with the first hint of interest in the dry voice.

'No. Nothing like that,' Bart told him.

He walked swiftly out back again thinking there was no other course but to return to the Kingston place. Then, as he neared the spot where the bay was tethered, he had a new thought. Perhaps he ought to carry the battle to the enemy. He had some cards up his sleeve yet. Maybe this was the time to play them. And he might as well start at the top. If he could interest Jim Malone in a proposition, he might still come out of this with a whole skin and a profit. His decision made, he mounted the bay and headed for the Ace Saloon.

Again he was forced to stick to the back streets and make his approach to the saloon from the rear. It was still bright daylight, and he kept his Stetson pulled well down over his forehead and hoped that no one would recognize him. Since it was a meal hour, there weren't too many moving about, and he was able to reach the back of the big building without attracting attention. He tied the bay to a convenient post, then entered the saloon through the rear door.

He had not been in this part of the building before, but he remembered the approximate location of Jim Malone's office from that other time. He was in a kind of dark vestibule with two doors leading from it. He chose the one on the right and edged it open a crack.

As he did so, he heard footsteps in the corridor on the other side; heavy footsteps that were moving rapidly in the other direction. Bart gave a sigh of relief. At least whoever it was had gone into the saloon rather than come out back where he was. All he had to do was wait until he was sure it was safe and then hope he'd find the fat Jim Malone in his office.

He rapidly considered what his approach to the saloon owner would be. He knew Jim Malone thought only in terms of profit. And it was on that he'd have to base his appeal for help. Maggie had made that clear to him.

Deciding he had waited long enough, he swung the door open the rest of the way and found himself at the opposite end of the same corridor down which he had marched with the saloon owner the other night. This meant the office would be the first on the right. Even though it was daylight, the corridor was shadowy. When he reached the door of the owner's office, it was partly ajar. Bart was almost sure this meant Jim Malone was inside.

He touched the handle and swung the door open. Sure enough, Malone was bent over his

121

desk, with a legal-looking document in front of him. He did not lift his head or pay the slightest attention to Bart as he entered.

Bart said, 'I'd like to talk to you, Malone.'

He waited, and still there was no answer. It was only then that the motionless figure at the desk began to give him an eerie feeling. All at once he sensed something was wrong. Advancing a couple of steps, he touched Malone's shoulder. The slight motion sent the heavy body falling forward on the desk, and he saw why the saloon owner hadn't responded to his coming. The knife buried to the hilt between his shoulder blades and the spreading red stain around it told the story. Jim Malone had been murdered!

CHAPTER NINE

It was a nightmarish situation. A moment ago Bart had hoped this meeting with Jim Malone might be the solution to his increasingly dangerous position. Now he found himself in an even less desirable situation than before. He eyed the slumped body of the dead political boss with shock and distaste.

This was something he had not expected. His mind moved rapidly as he sought to cope with his unexpected discovery. The knife protruding from Jim Malone's back appeared to be a type common in the country. He doubted if it would offer any significant lead as to who the killer might be. But one thing seemed certain. Whoever had committed the crime must have been known to the saloon owner and enough in his good graces so that he'd been able to stand by his chair and plunge the weapon into his back in an unsuspecting moment. Jim Malone had been stabbed to death by a henchman or crony!

It was as these thoughts came to him that his eye caught a gleam of yellow in the murdered man's right hand. Conquering a normal repugnance against touching the lifeless fingers, he opened them to retrieve a Mexican gold piece with a bullet hole directly through its center. It was an exact duplicate of the one the sheriff had found in the Kingston yard. This tied the murder with Texas Jack or had been placed there deliberately to do so.

And the citizens of Durez City were already suspicious that he was Texas Jack! Bart considered the gold piece grimly for a moment and then quickly thrust it in his pocket. He was about to leave when he heard the sound of heavy footsteps returning down the corridor. This meant a showdown!

It could be the killer, whom he'd heard leaving the office when he had been out back. But he doubted that. Probably this was one or the other of the saloon staff come to confer with Jim Malone. An even more unpleasant possibility struck him. It could be Maggie!

There was no way of escape. The tiny window was too small to offer an exit. As the footsteps approached the door, he drew his .45 and took a stand close to the wall and behind it. Whoever it was didn't pause to knock but swung the door open and came in. Bart waited only long enough to see the broad shoulders and black Stetson; then he brought the butt of the .45 down on the back of the intruder's head. The man gave a strangled gasp and dropped in his tracks. Only when he was sprawled on the floor did Bart recognize the unwelcome visitor as Sheriff Hill.

He didn't wait another minute. Making sure the corridor was clear, he let himself out and closed the door behind him. Then he retraced his steps through the rear exit, quickly untied and mounted the bay and rode off. This time he had no choice but to ride up the alley that ran the length of the Ace Saloon and emerge on the main street. He felt sure the few men standing in front of the saloon paid no attention as he headed the bay toward the other end of the town and Doc Webster's house.

If his luck was running, the Doc might be in. So far, things had been going against him today. But it seemed reasonable to expect them to change soon. When he reached the shabby house with its weathered picket fence, he headed the bay around to the back and in a moment was knocking at the rear door.

Miraculously it opened almost at once, and Doc peered out with a surprised look on his purple, bloated face. He frowned. 'You shouldn't be riding around until you've given that head a day or two to heal,' he said.

Bart brushed by him and, when he was in the middle of the dark kitchen, turned and said, 'Don't worry about that. There's plenty more to plague me now.'

Doc shut the door and came over to him. 'You seem like you've had a shock.'

'I have,' Bart said. 'I've just come from looking at a murdered man.'

The old man raised his eyebrows. 'Another one?'

Bart nodded grimly. 'Jim Malone!' And then he told him all that had happened.

'This is really bad,' Doc Webster worried.

Bart had made up his mind to say nothing about the gold piece he'd found in the murdered man's hand. He had his reasons for this, and they seemed strong enough to justify his holding back this information from even such a good friend as Doc Webster.

The two men stood facing each other in the dark, untidy room. Doc Webster ran a hand down his cheek. 'I saw Jim Malone not more than two hours ago. He was in the Round

125

Barrel, talking to someone I've never seen before.'

Bart was all attention. 'What did he look like?'

'Nothing special about him,' Doc said. 'He was middle-aged, thin, and looked kind of haggard, as if he had just finished a long ride.'

Bart listened, his good-looking face taking on a wary expression. 'You weren't close enough to hear what they were saying?'

Doc shook his head. 'No. But they seemed mighty serious. And after a while they left together.'

His lips pressed firmly closed and he nodded, as if arriving at some conclusion. Likely they went on to the Ace, and your stranger knifed him.'

'Could be,' the old man agreed. 'But why?'

'A lot of people might have liked to stick a knife in Malone's back,' Bart reminded him. 'This one saw the opportunity and took it.'

''Most everybody that hated Jim Malone lives right here in Durez City,' the old man said. 'Just because this stranger talked with him and they left the Round Barrel together doesn't mean he was the one who killed him.'

'That's true enough,' Bart agreed. 'But it must have happened soon after you saw them.'

Doc Webster frowned. 'This fellow had a sort of familiar look, and yet I'm certain I never met

126

him before. I don't make many mistakes about faces.'

'Apparently Jim Malone knew him.'

'I'd judge so, by the way they were hitting it off,' Doc said. 'They didn't look as if they had just met.'

'I have an idea they knew each other well enough.'

The old doctor gave him a surprised glance. 'What makes you so sure?'

'I'm figuring your stranger was the one who did it,' Bart explained. 'And whoever it was, Jim Malone gave him all the opportunity he needed. He couldn't have expected it to happen. So he must have known him well enough to trust him.'

'Which was a mistake,' Doc said quietly.

'Men like Jim Malone always make one sooner or later.'

There was a moment's silence between them. Through the dirty window Bart saw that darkness was closing in. By this time someone would have found the sheriff and Jim Malone's dead body. Or the sheriff himself would have come to and raised the alarm. Either way, by now the news must have spread that the saloon owner had been murdered. How long would it take for the sheriff to start tying up the murder with Bart?

Certainly not long if he hadn't removed that special bullet-scarred gold piece from Jim Malone's clenched fingers. This would have

127

definitely pointed suspicion his way. Now he might have a chance. But somewhere in Durez City there was a man who knew—the man who had killed Malone and left that gold piece there. And he would be wondering what had happened to it and who had taken it before the sheriff arrived. If he wondered long enough and tried to find out, he might give himself away, and then Bart would have the answer to many questions.

Doc interrupted his thoughts by asking, 'You had anything to eat?'

'No.' He didn't feel hungry, but he was suddenly aware of his great weariness.

'You're being real smart,' the old man scolded. 'Not bad enough to be on the go with that wound; you've given up eating as well.' He waved him to a chair. 'Sit down, and I'll rustle up something.'

Bart said, 'No. I don't want any food. I could use some coffee.'

'You can use more than that,' Doc said firmly, becoming the professional man again. Bart judged he hadn't been drinking much during the day.

Bart sat down and rolled himself a cigarette. Doc fussed around the kitchen, brought a small lamp and placed it in the center of the dish-cluttered table. The old man touched a match to the wick and returned the smoky shade in place. Bart could see the concern on the mottled face and figured Doc was doing plenty of thinking, although he wasn't saying much.

The old doctor cleared the table near him and put out a plate of bread and cheese, along with a mug of steaming coffee and the coffeepot. 'Get some of that inside you, son,' he ordered, and then sat in the chair at the end of the table to see that Bart did as he was told.

The coffee helped, and Bart soon found himself eating some of the bread and cheese. Even though he had no hunger, the food made him feel more human. He looked down the table and saw Doc's eyes studying him with a baffled light in them.

Bart said, 'You were right about the food.'

Doc nodded. 'Maybe you should listen to me regular instead of just when it strikes you.'

Bart gulped down some more of the hot coffee. 'Like when?'

'Like when you first came here, Bart,' the old man said, leaning forward earnestly. 'You went out of your way to help me, put yourself in bad with the sheriff and Malone. I wanted to pay you back. I tried to give you advice, but you wouldn't listen.'

Bart's pale blue eyes narrowed. 'There was nothing I could do.'

'You've let things happen ever since that first night,' Doc went on. 'From the time you went out to the Kingston place, you've deliberately let suspicion build about you. I could say you've actually encouraged it.'

'And you could be wrong.'

'I don't think so. You've refused to tell what happened to those old folks, so now most people think you murdered them.' He paused and sighed unhappily. 'Even I'm not sure. But I've liked you from the beginning, and I don't often make a mistake in a man.'

Bart sat back with a thin smile. 'Which means?'

'Maybe nothing,' the old man admitted. 'Maybe you are Texas Jack, come here to hole up from the federal men. And maybe you did kill the Kingstons and that big hombre who called you Texas Jack that night in the Ace Saloon.' He paused. 'Maybe you finished Jim Malone tonight and came here with a pack of lies.'

Bart said, 'Malone's man came back with the news the Kingstons aren't in Santa Ana.'

'I heard that early this afternoon,' Doc admitted. 'It sounded pretty bad for you.'

'I know. Eve Driscoll came by to warn me. She found me talking to Maggie Malone. She seemed to have the idea I was a murderer all over again.'

Doc Webster gave a low whistle. 'Those two females met at your place?'

'Yes.'

He scratched his head. 'Wonder they didn't

130

wind up tackling each other. Maggie and Eve
don't get on worth a tinker's dam.'

'It didn't come to that,' Bart said with a
rueful smile. 'But Maggie managed to upset her
pretty bad.'

The old doctor's face was suddenly serious.
'Poor Maggie!' he said. 'Wonder how she'll take
her Dad's murder?'

Bart shrugged. 'She shouldn't be
heartbroken. There was no love lost between
them.'

'Sometimes that doesn't matter,' Doc said.

'Maggie will manage,' Bart said confidently.
'That girl has spunk.'

'You like her?'

'Well enough.'

'So do I,' the old man said. 'I like her a
heap.' He glanced at Bart's empty plate. 'You
want some more bread and cheese?'

'No, thanks.' Bart stood up. 'I think I'll get
moving.'

Doc rose, too. 'You've got nothing to say to
me, Bart? Nothing to confess?'

Bart's face took on a hard expression. 'Not a
thing.'

'Where are you going?'

'I'm not planning to high-tail it,' Bart said. 'I
guess I'll just take a look around town.'

'Hadn't you better go back to the Kingston
place,' Doc urged. 'At least then you can alibi
you weren't here when it happened.'

131

'Might be worse. Somebody probably has seen me. And anyway, I called by the mayor's place before I went to the Ace. I talked with the clerk there and found the mayor had left town for St. Louis. So he could always come forward and say he saw me here.'

Doc Webster shook his head. 'I wish the mayor was here.'

'Does he go away like this often?'

'Every once in a while when he gets a yen for some new coffins,' Doc said with a grin on his grizzled features. 'Well, if you're going to size up the town, I might as well string along.'

Bart showed himself reluctant to take the old man with him. 'There may be trouble,' he warned.

'All the more reason I should go,' Doc said, putting on his worn hat. 'And don't forget you're in no shape to mix up in any fights.'

'I'll remember,' Bart said.

They moved to the door together, and Doc faced him and asked, 'Where do you aim to go first?'

'You saw this stranger in the Round Barrel earlier,' Bart said. 'Maybe we'll have luck and find him there again.'

'I doubt it,' Doc said, 'especially if he's the one who did it.'

'Won't hurt to see,' Bart told him. And they went out.

The news of the murder must have swept

through Durez City like wildfire. Jim Malone was really boss man of the cow town, and his violent end was causing excitement. When Bart and Doc Webster entered the Round Barrel, it was crowded and all the talk seemed to be concentrated on the murder. There were so many people in the place and the air was so blue with smoke it was impossible to pick anyone out quickly. Bart and Doc Webster elbowed their way through to the bar at a spot near the door and waited for one of the busy bartenders to take their orders.

Doc glanced down the bar. 'A lot of thirsty cowpokes tonight,' he said.

Bart nodded. 'Judging from what I hear, most of them are trying to be amateur detectives.'

Suddenly Doc Webster plucked his arm excitedly. 'Down at the lower end of the bar! I see that thin fellow, the one that talked with Malone this afternoon.'

Bart leaned forward and observed the man. He had a mean hatchet face that made him look older than he probably was, and he wasn't talking to anyone; just standing there sullenly with a drink in front of him.

'Looks like our man,' Bart said. 'I want to talk to him.'

Doc's bloated face was a study in despair. 'You hadn't ought to get in any row until that head mends.'

'I don't aim to row with him,' Bart said quietly. 'I just want to ask him a few questions.' And with that he stepped away from his place at the bar and started down toward the other end. Doc followed close at his heels.

He'd only gone a half-dozen steps when he saw a cowboy at the bar nudge another, who at once turned around to glare at him malevolently. It was Nick Cressy, his cheek taped with a bandage as a result of their fight in front of the Ace Saloon. The dandified foreman didn't say anything, but Bart saw his hand instantly reach for the bottle before him on the bar. Doc Webster gave a sharp cry of warning as Nick brought the bottle down in a glancing blow on Bart's shoulder. As Bart dodged quickly, the bottle was shattered against the bar. By this time everyone around the two men were alerted that a return battle was about to take place, and they drifted back from them to form a circle.

'Get away from here, Bart!' Doc Webster ordered forlornly from the sidelines.

Bart didn't bother to reply.

'Mean hombre, ain't you?' Nick grated between clenched teeth.

Then he made a lunge at Bart with a direct right that caught him a glancing blow on the jaw. Bart took advantage of his nearness to land a left and a right to Nick's face. On the second blow blood spurted from the bandaged area,

134

and Nick grunted and stumbled back.

The crowd was roaring: 'Fight! Fight!' And each moment the ring of onlookers grew. Bart vaguely heard Doc in the background still begging him to quit and run. But that was crazy advice now.

A snarl of hate came from Nick's throat as he crouched forward, right hand reaching for his six-shooter. Bart took one step forward. His left hand shot out and intercepted his adversary's gun hand, and with the same neat trick he'd used on the beady-eyed man, he caught the arm up behind Nick's back and exerted pressure until the dark-haired man's eyes bulged and sweat came out at his temples. A sudden laugh went up from the men crowding around.

Bart spoke close to Nick's ear. 'I can break your arm if I want to,' he said. 'And I will if you try anything like reaching for your shooting iron again.'

The veins stood out at Nick's temples, and he nodded to show he understood.

Just as Bart was about to release him, he felt something round and hard jabbed against his backbone. And he heard Sheriff Hill's cold voice: 'Raise them, mister. Raise them fast.'

Bart stiffened and raised his arms. And as he did so, from the corner of his eye he noticed the hatchet-faced man dodge out the swinging doors of the saloon.

The foreman of the Diamond O had

135

recovered himself now and was smiling in triumph at the timely arrival of the sheriff. He stood facing Bart, his henchmen crowding around him. Doc Webster stood uncertainly watching the proceedings a few feet farther back.

'I reckon you won't be startin' any more brawls for a while,' Sheriff Hill said, the gun still pressed against Bart.

'What's the charge, Sheriff?' Bart asked coolly.

'Murder. More than one of them. The Kingstons and now Jim Malone.'

'You can't make those charges stick,' Bart warned him.

'I might surprise you, Mister Landry,' Sheriff Hill said. 'Now march, and no tricks.'

The crowd parted to let them walk through. Doc Webster had made no attempt to come along and now was far behind.

The sheriff kept the gun pressed close to Bart all the way to the Durez City jailhouse. And Bart knew better than to make a break for it, since he guessed the square-faced representative of the law would like nothing better than to drill him as he was trying to get away and call the case closed.

The Durez City jail, a one-story stone building with the sheriff's office in the front and three cells in the rear, was not imposing. As soon as they got there, Sheriff Hill instructed his deputy to slip handcuffs on Bart and hook one of them on the chair in which he sat to be questioned.

Bart smiled up at the sheriff. 'Mind giving me a smoke? It's awkward rolling one when I'm handcuffed this way.'

The sheriff glared at him. 'I'll bet you've rolled plenty of them in the saddle with one hand on the reins,' he said. But nevertheless he gave Bart a cigarette and even lighted it for him. 'The service here suit you?'

'It'll do. I won't be here long,' Bart said, taking a deep draw on the cigarette and exhaling the smoke lazily.

'The devil you won't,' Sheriff Hill told him angrily. 'When you leave here, it will be to stand trial in City Hall. And this time you won't have the mayor on your side. You won't have anyone!'

Bart smiled. 'Don't be too sure! There may be someone on his way here right now.'

It was purely a bluff on his part, a move to stall for time and prevent the sheriff from knowing he was actually worried. But it worked with surprising success. The sheriff looked nervously toward the door and then turned to his deputy, who was standing by Bart's chair.

'Better close that door and put the bolt in place,' he told him in a shaky voice. 'We don't want to risk any of Texas Jack's gang forcing their way in here.'

137

'Yes, sir,' the deputy said, and hurried to carry out the instructions with almost comic haste.

Bart laughed softly. He decided to play the thing for all it was worth. 'You're mighty upset, Sheriff. And I always understood Texas Jack worked alone, that he didn't have a gang.'

'Don't you worry,' Sheriff Hill told him. 'It don't matter whether you're Texas Jack or not. Your neck is going to stretch just the same.'

'You can't convict me without some evidence,' Bart told him.

'We know the Kingstons ain't alive,' Sheriff Hill snapped. 'They never showed up in Santa Ana.'

'Which doesn't prove they are dead.'

'It proves enough.' The sheriff pointed a stubby finger at him, his square face distorted with rage. 'You've made a fool of me for the last time. You ain't ever goin' to be turned loose in a breathin' condition.'

'There must be some law left in Durez City,' Bart said. 'You can't hang me because it suits you.'

'Maybe I can't and maybe I can.' The sheriff pushed his ugly face close to Bart's, so close he could smell the squat man's foul breath. 'I knowed from the time you got here and holed up in the Kingston house that you were on the wrong side of the law.'

'On the wrong side of your kind of law,' Bart

138

corrected him.

'All the town has been talking about you and what happened to the Kingstons. And because Jim Malone proved you were lying, you came to town and killed him!'

'So far you've just made accusations,' Bart reminded him. 'You haven't proven anything. If the Kingstons are dead, murdered by me, what did I do with the bodies?'

Sheriff Hill straightened up, and an ugly smile crossed his square face. 'I don't think it will take too long to turn them up. I'm sending some men out to the farm tomorrow, and they'll dig up every inch of that place until they locate them.'

This hit Bart hard. He knew once they came to that area he'd covered with lumber, there would be no keeping his secret any longer. But he didn't let the sheriff see his sudden surge of fear.

Instead he smiled again and said, 'You'll just make yourself ridiculous, Sheriff. I'm warning you.'

'You ain't in any position to warn anybody,' the sheriff said. 'It won't even help you to make a confession.'

'I have nothing to confess.'

'Just now you hinted you was Texas Jack,' the sheriff said with a greedy expression on his ugly face. 'You know there's a heap of reward money being offered for Texas, dead or alive.

139

The way I see it, you're going to hang anyway. So why not confess and give me and Miller a chance to get some of that heavy cash?'

Bart would have found the clumsy overture funny if he hadn't been in such a tight spot.

He asked, 'What would that get me?'

Sheriff Hill's pig eyes fixed on him eagerly. 'Me and the deputy could make it mighty pleasant for you while you're waitin' for trial and afterward until the hanging. Or we can do just the opposite if you don't want to go along with us.'

Bart pretended to think it over. 'That's a mighty tempting offer, Sheriff,' he said seriously. 'There's just one thing wrong with it.'

'What's that?' the Sheriff wanted to know.

'I don't happen to be Texas Jack,' Bart said.

CHAPTER TEN

The sheriff regarded him with rage for a moment. Then he jeered, 'You may change your tune before we're finished with you, Mister Landry.'

'And you may find yourself without a job when Mayor Peters gets back,' Bart told him. 'Doc Webster will tell him what went on.'

The sheriff laughed. 'Who'll listen to that old drunk?'

'The mayor, for one,' Bart said. 'And there must be other decent citizens in town who weren't paid off by Malone like you and your crowd.'

The sheriff's square face grew crimson. 'You better go a mite easy with that tongue or wind up swallowing some teeth!' He shoved a big fist menacingly towards Bart's face.

Bart was on the point of making a reply when there came a heavy pounding on the jailhouse door. The sheriff stepped back as if he'd been touched by flame, and his ugly face paled as he stared at the door. Bart saw the crooked lawman had already decided a gang of Texas Jack's men were outside, ready to rescue him.

The deputy who was standing nearest the door gave the sheriff a worried glance. 'What'll I do?' he wanted to know.

The sheriff signaled him to remain where he was. 'Wait and see,' he said.

Bart was enjoying it all, although he had no idea who might be out there. He smiled. 'Not nervous, are you, Sheriff?'

The ugly man scowled at him in answer. Then the pounding on the door was repeated. And this time a familiar voice called: 'Let us in! I demand you open this door!'

Bart settled back in his chair. It was Doc Webster who was raising the racket.

The sheriff gave Bart a smug glance and

141

nodded for the deputy to open the door with a wise smile on his square face. But when the door was opened and Maggie Malone came in with Doc Webster, his smile vanished.

'You shouldn't be out around tonight, Miss Maggie,' the sheriff remonstrated in what was meant to be a paternal tone.

The blonde girl looked at him. 'I'm all right,' she said in a strangely quiet voice. Bart saw that she was pale and her eyes red from crying. But otherwise she seemed unshaken by her father's murder.

Doc rushed over to Bart anxiously. 'You all right, son?'

He nodded. 'I'm glad you came through.'

'I had to get Maggie,' the old man said. And then defiantly to the sheriff: 'She's got something to tell you, Mister Lawman.'

The sheriff wet his lips nervously as if expecting trouble and gave Maggie an uneasy glance. 'What's this all about?' he wanted to know.

Maggie sighed. 'Let Bart go.'

'What's that?'

'You heard me,' she went on in the same weary tone.

'You must be plumb hysterical!' the sheriff blustered.

'I'm not hysterical, and I mean what I said,' Maggie told him in her old forceful way.

'But he killed your Pa!'

142

Doc stepped forward toward the angry man. 'That's a large statement, Sheriff. Can you prove it?'

'It'll be settled in court!' the sheriff promised.

'No, it won't,' Maggie objected, 'because Bart isn't going to go before any court. He didn't kill my father. I did.'

There was a long moment of shocked silence in the room. Even Bart was stunned. But of course he knew at once Maggie was lying to save him.

Bart spoke out at once. 'There's no need of that, Maggie. I'll get out of this without you taking the blame.'

She came over to him and put a hand on his shoulder, her pretty face solemn. 'I told the sheriff the truth. I killed my father.'

Doc stared at her. 'You know what you're saying, girl?'

'This is awful, Miss Maggie,' the sheriff moaned, finally finding his voice. 'What are folks in town going to say?'

'What they've always said and known,' Maggie said, her pert chin stuck out. 'That I hated Jim Malone, even though he was my father. They won't be too surprised at what I've done.'

The sheriff removed his stetson and wiped his forehead with a bright bandana. 'This is terrible! What am I going to do about you? I

143

know Jim wouldn't want to see you locked up, no matter what you did.'

'Place her in my custody,' Doc said importantly. 'I'll look after her until the mayor returns. I'll see she gets proper treatment.'

The sheriff rubbed his chin. Bart could see the idea appealed to him, but there were still obstacles. The sheriff confirmed this by saying, 'What'll I tell folks meanwhile? Everyone knows I've arrested this fella here.'

'Tell them you made a mistake,' Doc said. 'And you did. You have nothing to hold him with on either of these charges.'

The sheriff gave a great sigh. 'I don't know what to say. I'm too mixed up. I don't like lettin' this hombre loose.'

Bart said, 'I'm not going anywhere. You can locate me any time you want at the Kingston place.'

Sheriff Hill shook his head. 'I never thought I'd live to see the day.' He gave Maggie a woeful look. 'You sure got us all in a lovely fix, Miss Maggie.'

'I know,' she said, her head down. 'I'm sorry.'

'You willin' to go with Doc until the court calls you?'

She nodded. 'I don't care what happens. I'll do anything you say.'

'Then I guess that settles it,' the sheriff said, rising like an old man. 'I don't know what

144

things in Durez City are comin' to!' He nodded to the deputy. 'Let Mister Landry go.'

The deputy, who also seemed dazed, came over and unlocked the handcuff that was holding Bart. Then he stepped back quickly as if he had an idea Bart might take a swing at him.

'I told you I wouldn't be here long.' Bart smiled at the sheriff.

The burly man pointed a finger at him. 'Don't think you're in the clear,' he said. 'I'm sending men out to the Kingston place tomorrow like I said. And if we don't find those corpus delecti the Doc is so worried about, I'll miss my guess.'

'Send them any time, Sheriff,' Bart said lightly. 'I'll serve them coffee.'

Doc gave him a warning glance that begged him not to overdo it. And with a nod toward the sheriff, he took Maggie Malone by the arm and said, 'With your permission, I'll take my patient home with me at once. I want to begin treating her for what was clearly temporary insanity.'

The sheriff scowled. 'I'll be coming by every day to check on how you're doing.' He paused as a new idea hit him. 'Folks will be expecting a bang-up funeral for Jim. Will she be able to attend?'

'Under my care,' the doctor said importantly. 'I'll escort her.'

145

'Meanwhile you go easy on the brandy,' the sheriff warned him.

'Are you suggesting I'm not fully competent, Sheriff?' Doc Webster demanded, his mottled face registering high indignation.

Sheriff Hill gave him a nasty grin. 'I only know folks had a new doctor come to take over your practice. Maybe they just thought it was time you should retire!'

Doc led Maggie to the door. 'Come along, my dear,' he said. 'We will not remain to hear this uncouth humor!'

Bart went along with them. The three of them walked slowly away from the lights of the jailhouse. When they were a good distance from the building, Maggie stopped and turned to Doc Webster in the darkness.

'All right, Doc,' she said in a tired voice. 'You can go now.'

'But, Maggie, I gave my word. You're my patient!' the old man protested.

'We all know that was just a show,' she went on in the same dull tone. 'I didn't kill Dad. I only told the sheriff that to get Bart off. Now I want to talk to him alone.'

'But, Maggie, you heard the sheriff say he would come by my place!' Bart couldn't see the old man's features clearly as he continued to argue, but he was certain he was very upset.

'I'll see about that,' she told him. 'I'll call by in the morning. Don't worry about it.'

146

The old man hesitated. 'You'll be all right?'

'I'll see she gets home safely,' Bart promised.

Doc still seemed unwilling to leave. 'I don't know,' he said. 'I'm worried about you both.'

'You needn't be,' Maggie said with some annoyance. 'Now please go.'

Bart saw the old man stand in silence a moment longer, then bow his head and turn to go the other way. Maggie watched him vanish into the darkness before she turned to face Bart.

'Now you can go, too,' she said abruptly.

Bart reached out and touched her arm. 'Maggie, I don't understand.'

She pulled back from him. 'There's nothing to understand,' she said unhappily. 'I want you to leave while you still have a chance.'

'Not before I thank you for what you've done,' he said, 'and tell you how sorry I am about your father. I know it leaves you very much alone.'

'Don't bother with all that!' Her words ended in what sounded suspiciously like a sob.

Bart stepped near her again, vainly trying to see her face in the heavy shadows. 'Maggie, I'm your friend!'

'I pick my friends!' she said. 'And I don't choose murderers!'

'What are you saying?'

'I saw you!'

'Saw me what?'

'Leave my father's office after you killed him.

147

I went in right afterward and found him and the sheriff. But I didn't let on I saw you.'

Bart was now aware why she was behaving so oddly. He spoke in a low, urgent tone. 'Listen to me, Maggie. And please believe me. I do admit I was in the office. I had to knock out the sheriff to get away. But I didn't kill your father. He was dead when I got there.'

'It's all right,' she said dully. 'You don't have to lie. I'm willing to take the blame.'

'But you mustn't,' he implored her. 'Not for me! I'm not the guilty one. I found a gold coin in his hand, a special coin, the kind Texas Jack always leaves at the scene of a killing.'

'Folks think you are Texas Jack.'

Bart began to feel he was facing hopeless odds in trying to clear himself in her eyes. He said, 'Maggie, you're a wonderful girl. I don't know I've ever met anyone like you.'

'How about Eve Driscoll? She's more your type!' Maggie's tone was hard.

'Let's leave Eve out of this,' he said.

'Let's leave everything out of it,' Maggie told him sharply. 'I hated my father. I know that was wrong now. But it's too late. The thing that counts is that he was no good! I knew it! You knew it! Every decent person in Durez City knew it!'

'Nothing can be gained by going over that,' he said.

'I want you to understand,' she told him. 'I

148

don't consider my father's life worth another man's; not even yours. So this way I'm squaring things all around. I'll take the blame, and you clear out!'

'Not before I make you realize I've told you the truth.'

'I'm sick of truth, Bart,' she said, sounding as if she were physically ill. 'Just walk away and leave me, or I'm going back to the jail and tell the sheriff I saw you coming out of the office after you did it.'

'There's no other choice?' he asked.

'None.'

Her tone was definite. He sighed. 'All right, Maggie. I'll go now, as you ask. But before I leave Durez City, I'll prove I didn't kill your father.'

Her answer was to turn away from him and begin to walk slowly back toward the jail. He knew she wasn't likely to make idle threats. Unless he left at once, she'd tell the sheriff what she believed to be the true account of events. And he knew the burly lawman would be only too eager to accept it.

He hurried off to where he'd tied the bay near the entrance of the Round Barrel Saloon. Things had quieted down since the sheriff had marched him out, and he was able to reach the horse and ride off without anyone noticing him. He was still deeply troubled by Maggie's behavior and shocked that she should so readily

149

believe he was a killer.

He rode back to the house with the picket fence and saw there was a light in the kitchen. Luckily the doctor had gone straight home and not to one of the saloons, as Bart had feared. He jumped down from the bay and hurried to the back door, eager to talk to the old man.

But when he opened the door, the picture he saw filled him with dismay. Doc was standing by the cluttered table, with a liquor bottle to his mouth, head tilted back as he drank the fiery contents straight. Hearing Bart come in, he put the bottle down.

He stared at Bart stupidly. 'Thought you were with Maggie,' he said in a thick voice.

'We had a row,' Bart said in a sharp tone. 'She thinks I killed her father.'

Doc blinked at him. 'And she still took the blame herself?'

He nodded. 'She has some crazy reason; something to do with her father being rotten and deserving what he got.'

'Which is true,' Doc Webster said with drunken dignity.

'But not the way she has it confused in her mind,' Bart said. 'You've got to see her and talk to her for me; try and make her understand.'

Doc swayed slightly. 'Trouble is I don't know.'

'Don't know what?' Bart felt himself growing angry.

150

The old man smiled drunkenly. 'I don't know anything. Who you are, what you've done, or whether you did kill Jim Malone!' And he lifted the bottle to his lips again.

Bart's anger reached a peak, and he grabbed the bottle and hurled it to the floor, where it shattered. Doc Webster's mottled face was startled, and Bart hoped he might have sobered him. The old man stood in stunned silence, staring at Bart and not speaking.

Then he said, 'I'm sorry I ever laid eyes on you, Bart. You've brought new evil to this place.'

'What are you raving about?' Bart demanded irritably.

'There's a darkness around you,' the doctor went on. 'And you've drawn us all into it. Go away from here, Bart! Just go away!'

Bart stared at the old man, who turned and stumbled off through the doorway leading to another room, leaving Bart alone. It was a shocking end to their brief friendship. Bart stared after him for a long moment, then, with a sigh, made his way to the rear door and out.

The night was cold again as he rode the bay back to the Kingston place. And he was filled with an inner chill that came from the knowledge that the two people he liked best in Durez City had turned against him. He knew that he shouldn't have been surprised. He had chosen this solitary way of life, and now he was

151

paying the price for it.

Everything was quiet at the Kingston place when he rode up. He took the bay into the stable and looked after it. Nick Cressy hadn't bothered to send any thugs to try to shoot him down this time, and Jim Malone was dead and cold in Mayor Peters' undertaking parlor. There had been a few changes. And they included the loss of Maggie and the Doc as friends.

He opened the back door and went into the kitchen. The same dead smell that had bothered him in the Kingston place from the beginning hit his nostrils in a sickening wave now. The house had been shut up since he had left late in the afternoon to look up Mayor Peters and found himself catapulted into one scrape after another. Making his way through the darkness to the table, he reached in his pocket for a match and, striking it, touched its flame to the lamp wick. Only as he put back the glass shade did he see the figure seated in the chair across the room with a Colt pointed straight at him.

It was the hatchet-faced man he'd seen in the bar, the one Doc had told him had been talking to Jim Malone before he was killed. Now the pale hatchet face beneath the big hat smiled at him nastily.

'You kept me waiting a long time, Landry,' the stranger said. 'Just reach for the ceiling.'

Bart lifted his hands as he stared at the thin

man and repeated the words the Kingstons had said to him on the night of his arrival. 'So you've come!'

The hatchet-faced one nodded as he came over and snapped Bart's .45 from its holster and stepped back. 'I've come.'

'I figured you would.'

'You knew I had to,' the other said with an edge in his voice. 'You been having yourself quite a time.'

'It's been quiet,' Bart said, his hands still up as the blue muzzle of the Colt stared at him.

'Not all that quiet,' the stranger said. 'Folks around here think you're Texas Jack.'

'I can't help what they think,' Bart said.

The stranger laughed again. 'Don't try to fool me, Landry. You been encouraging it. I know you've acted like you were Texas Jack in a couple of other towns as well. Big Mike believed you were the real thing.'

'Big Mike?'

The stranger's hatchet-face went hard. 'You remember. You broke his arm and left him. Then I came by and finished the job for you.'

'So you were the one who drilled him?'

'That's right.'

'Why?'

'He wasn't useful any more.'

'That's a good reason.'

The stranger smiled crookedly again. 'The best.'

153

'What about Jim Malone?'

The eyes of the stranger narrowed. 'He got special attention. Malone was getting too big for Durez City. Too ambitious!'

'Texas Jack left his calling card when he knifed him,' Bart said. 'I happened to find it.'

'And now we come to you,' the stranger said, never allowing the Colt to waver.

'I'm not important,' Bart said.

'Oh, you're wrong about that!' The stranger moved a step to the right, and his shadow played against the wall in the dim glow of the lamplight. 'Where are the Kingstons?'

'Your mother and father?' Bart asked coolly.

The hatchet-face looked sick. Then the crooked smile returned. 'So you know about that. All right; where are my folks?'

'They're a long way off.'

'You finished them?' There was curiosity rather than condemnation in the question.

'Would that really bother you much?' Bart asked scornfully.

Hatchet-face's eyes narrowed to nasty slits. 'Not too much,' he said, 'especially since they ratted on me!'

'Your parents are decent people.'

'They told you where the stuff was hidden.' The stranger's voice became angry and rose slightly as he went on. 'They sent for you and told you all about it.'

'What if they did?'

'Then I don't care what happened to them,' the stranger snapped. 'Where is the stuff? Not where I buried it. I looked under that lumber you put out to cover the place where you dug it up.'

Bart smiled at him. 'I've been waiting for you to come and find that it was gone.'

'There was enough gold down there to set a man up in Mexico for life,' the stranger said. 'Where is it?'

'You don't really expect me to tell you?'

The stranger came closer and lifted the Colt menacingly. 'I'll give you a slow count of three to remember,' he said.

CHAPTER ELEVEN

Bart let his eyes move from the hard face to the muzzle of the gun. He knew the stranger meant what he said. This man was mean and a killer. So this could be the end of the trail. It had all come to nothing, in spite of everything he'd tried to do.

'I'm waiting,' the hatchet-faced man said, and began his count. 'One—'

But he got no further, for suddenly there was the sound of a rider coming into the yard. The stranger kept the Colt on Bart but sidled across the kitchen to put aside the curtain and peer

155

out. Then he moved back quickly and said, 'Someone is coming in here. I'm going inside. I don't want you to say anything or try anything. Just act natural and get rid of whoever it is fast, or I'll drill you both!'

Without waiting for a reply, the stranger backed into the small bedroom adjoining the kitchen, where he could stand in the shadows and still keep Bart and his visitor fully covered. Bart remained motionless, waiting to see who it might be, and hoping this would offer some means of escape.

The door opened, and when he saw who it was his hopes sank. Maggie Malone came toward him, remorse showing on her lovely face. She threw her arms around him and began to sob, her face pressed close to his chest.

'Bart, forgive me! I don't know how I could have behaved as I did a while ago. I was so upset. I don't believe you killed my father, no matter what I saw. I don't believe you'd murder anyone.'

He was unprepared for this sudden change of attitude on her part. Putting his arms about her, he awkwardly tried to offer some comfort. 'Don't let it worry you,' he said. 'I understood. I understand now.'

She gave a deep sigh, her head still close to his. 'I began to think about it after you left,' she said. 'I couldn't believe I'd acted the way I had.

156

There was nothing to do but come here and apologize.'

'You shouldn't be out riding alone at this time of night,' he cautioned her.

Maggie looked up at him with the ghost of a smile. 'I've never had anyone bother me yet.'

'There's always a first time,' Bart warned her.

Her expression became troubled. 'You're acting strange, Bart. Have I hurt you so badly? Can't you forgive me?'

He shook his head. 'Of course you're forgiven.'

'But your face is so drawn. And you're so quiet, not like yourself!'

Bart sighed. 'I'm tired. It's been a bad day. You'd better go straight back to town.'

Maggie drew away to study him more objectively. Her lovely blue eyes mirrored her alarm. 'Something is wrong,' she announced. 'I know it.'

He attempted a smile. 'Maggie, must you always be so obstinate? I've told you to ride back to Durez City. I'd go with you, I should go with you, but I have to wait for someone here.'

'Who?'

'No one you know.'

A stubborn expression crossed Maggie's face, and the pert jaw jutted out in a way all too familiar to him. He knew he was going to have trouble handling her. And if he didn't send her on her way, she'd also be at the mercy of the

157

mad killer in the next room.

She went over and sat on one of the plain kitchen chairs, her hands in her lap, her blue eyes fixed on him. 'I'm not moving from here until you tell me what this is all about.'

He took a step toward her and halted, fearing he might alert the trigger finger on the Colt into action. 'Maggie, be reasonable for once,' he begged.

'Not until you tell me what's going on. I'm sure it has to do with what happened in town tonight.'

'I want you to go home where you'll be safe,' he insisted, coming as close to the truth as he dared.

He was relieved of the necessity to act a part any longer when the hatchet-faced man made his entrance from the bedroom, gun in hand. Maggie gave a gasp and looked at Bart with fear in her lovely eyes. She didn't attempt to move.

Bart said, 'I told you there was always a first time. Now I'm afraid you're in this with me.'

'I'll do the talking here,' the stranger told him in his hard voice. And to Maggie, 'You're just a little too curious for your own good, Miss Malone.'

'Who are you?' she asked.

He gave a nasty chuckle. 'I wouldn't be surprised if I'm the only one with a right to be here. That is, if Landry finished off my folks as everyone says.'

158

Maggie appealed to Bart. 'What's he talking about?'

'He's the Kingstons' dead son,' Bart said, knowing that he was taking a risk of arousing the outlaw's anger by continuing to talk, but also aware that each word he said was giving them that much more time. 'Only he didn't die. He became an outlaw before they moved here. They had nothing to do with him nor he with them, until one day it suited him to hide some hidden loot here.'

'Gold, Miss Malone,' the stranger said harshly. 'Lots of it. And unless your friend comes across and tells me what's happened to it fast, both you and he are going to have a very short future.'

'Is this true, Bart?' she asked.

'The gold is gone, along with his folks,' Bart said.

The stranger moved toward Bart. 'You'll never get away with this double-cross. I'll find that gold, and I'll locate them after you've stopped breathing. You're nothing but a tinhorn outlaw yourself, going around pretending to be Texas Jack.'

Maggie surprised Bart by directing her next question to the stranger. 'Then he isn't Texas Jack?'

The hatchet-faced man gave a mean laugh. 'You must be kidding! Him!'

'And you are,' she said with one of her surprise reversals.

The stranger looked more than a little taken back, but he recovered enough to say, 'That doesn't happen to be any of your business, Miss Malone.'

But this didn't feaze Maggie. She continued to stare the outlaw down, with loathing on her pretty face. 'And you killed my father. I'm sure you did!'

The stranger made no comment other than a crooked smile. He turned his attention to Bart. 'I haven't much more time,' he said. 'There's also your girl friend to consider now. Either you talk or I'll drill you both.'

'You won't be any better off after that,' Bart told him.

'I'll be a lot more satisfied,' the stranger said.

'Why don't you tell him, Bart?' Maggie asked.

'Because it wouldn't do any good. He'd shoot us anyway as soon as he got the information.'

The stranger turned to Maggie. 'Don't pay any attention to that talk. I'm willing to make a deal.'

Bart shook his head. 'I'm not. I promised your folks protection, and they're going to have it.'

'I'll not do anything to them,' the stranger promised. 'After all, they are my folks.'

'I know how you treated them when you first came back,' Bart said, 'how you cowed them into silence for months until they had the courage to send for me. Your word isn't any good.'

The finger on the trigger of the Colt moved ominously. 'Maybe we've talked long enough,' the stranger grated.

'Let her go, and I'll make a deal,' Bart offered quickly.

The stranger shook his head. 'No dice. I can't risk that.'

Maggie was in a subdued mood now. 'Don't worry about me,' she said. 'Anyway, you were right. You can't trust his word.'

There was a moment of silence. Bart was about to plead for Maggie's release again when, some distance off, he was certain he heard a sound. He hesitated, and then he was sure. It was the sound of carriage wheels. Involuntarily he glanced toward the stranger to see if he had heard. He had! The thin body of the hatchet-faced man went tense, and he glared at Bart and Maggie.

'Don't either of you make a move or a sound,' he warned. And then he dived for the kitchen window to see who it was. 'We've got all the company we can handle right now,' he said in a low, angry tone. 'This one gets the treatment outside.' And he poked the muzzle of the Colt through the glass so he would have clear shooting when the moment came.

The carriage continued to approach the old

161

house in the darkness. And the three of them waited tensely in the faint amber glow of the small lamp. The stranger's cruel face was etched in its glow as he leaned by the window, his gun ready. Maggie and Bart, in turn, kept their gaze fixed on him. Bart worried that the driver of the carriage might be Doc Webster. If so, the old man's chances of surviving were slim.

But then Doc never drove a carriage. He always rode out.

Then Bart became aware that something odd had happened. The carriage had not turned into the yard as they'd all expected. There was only silence now. It must have gone on or stopped out front. Bart began to speculate wildly.

Then, from behind him, a familiar voice spoke in a quiet tone. 'You at the window, sir, will you kindly drop that Colt? I happen to have you nicely covered with a weapon of my own, and I'm not inclined to wait. Now, please!'

The hatchet-faced man let the gun clatter to the floor and, raising his hands, turned toward the newcomer with a fear-stricken expression on his pale face. Bart turned as well and with a great surge of relief saw that it was none other than Mayor Peters.

'Mayor! I thought you were away,' Bart exclaimed.

The mayor looked as lugubrious as ever. His bloodhound face was set in mournful lines, but

162

his gun hand held the six-shooter pointed at the stranger. He said, ' I came back unexpectedly. And while I detest violence of all sorts, I saw that I must resort to it here.'

'You handled it right by coming in the front,' Bart told him. 'How did you know we were in trouble?'

'I have great intuition,' the mayor said in a melancholy tone. 'I thought there seemed to be something odd here and decided to investigate before I revealed myself.' He looked in Maggie's direction. 'I know about your father, my dear. My sympathy goes out to you.'

Maggie was on her feet now. 'This man killed my father, Mayor!'

'Really?' The mayor sounded doubtful as he stared at the stranger. 'Who is he?'

Bart spoke up. 'A renegade son of the Kingstons. Buried gold here. I came to straighten things out at the old folks' request. They were frightened and caught between him and the law.'

The hound-dog face regarded him sadly. 'Now I understand your presence in Durez City, sir. You are a lawman.'

Bart smiled. 'Federal marshal, sir. I've been on the track of Texas Jack for more than a year. The trail led here.' He turned to the hatchet-faced man. 'And to him.'

'I see,' the mayor said. 'Then I can assure

163

you of Sheriff Hill's assistance. Where are the Kingstons?'

'About two miles from here in a hunting lodge at Willow Ridge. They promised to keep out of sight until all this was settled.'

The mayor nodded. 'And of course that clears you of any suspicion of murder. Excellent, Marshal Landry. The townspeople have been convinced you were a killer. But neither Doctor Webster nor I agreed.'

'Thanks for your confidence in me,' Bart said, flashing a grateful smile toward Mayor Peters. Then he looked Maggie's way. 'And for yours as well.'

The lovely blue eyes had a new light of tenderness in them. 'I only doubted you for a few minutes,' she said.

'That didn't count,' he assured her. Then, turning to the mayor: 'I'll get this fellow's gun and take back my own. Then I'll take him into town.' He took a step toward the hatchet-faced man.

'One moment,' the mayor said.

Bart was surprised at the urgency in his voice. He turned to see what the reason was; he was now only a few feet from the stranger and the Colt that still lay on the floor. He said, 'Yes?'

'What about Miss Malone? She has known enough violence and tragedy for one night. She must be safely escorted home,' the mayor said.

Bart smiled. 'Sure,' he replied. 'She had

better go with you.'

'Very well,' the mayor agreed, still covering the stranger with his six-shooter. 'And what about the gold? Is it still hidden here?'

Bart shook his head. 'No. It's safe at Willow Ridge with the Kingstons.'

'Excellent, Marshal Landry,' the mayor said, and Bart was startled to see a smile cross the hound-dog features for the first time in his memory. 'You have been extremely helpful.'

Bart frowned. 'I don't follow you.' He turned and saw that the hatchet-faced man was holding his Colt again, pointed at him. He grinned at Bart.

'The fact is,' Mayor Peters said in a quite different tone, sharper and without the assumed melancholy, 'this young man and I are much better friends than you guessed.'

Bart looked at the mayor, saw the six-shooter still in his hand and knew at that moment the gun had been intended for him and Maggie from the start, not for the stranger. The mayor's entrance had not been a surprise, but carefully arranged. And he had fallen for the dodge. Suddenly it came to him who Mayor Peters really was.

Hating himself for what he could only regard as his blind stupidity, he surrendered to an impulse. Reaching into his vest pocket, he drew out the Mexican gold piece with the bullet hole in it that he'd found in Jim Malone's hand and

165

tossed it contemptuously at the feet of the mayor.

'That belongs to you,' he said quietly.

'No, Bart!' It was Maggie who cried out the words incredulously as her eyes questioned him.

He nodded to her. 'I've been pretty stupid. He's the one who killed your father and the others. Meet Texas Jack.'

Mayor Peters smiled again. And somehow the smile didn't seem to fit the doleful face. 'I'm sorry we are not meeting under happier circumstances, Miss Malone. I've always admired you. Now I offer you my personal good wishes.'

The stranger spoke up. 'We'd better move fast, Boss!'

The mayor nodded, suddenly looking incongruous in his dark suit and hat, hardly the garb of a desperately wanted outlaw. But this convenient dual personality had been his protection. And his absences from Durez City to order coffins had provided him with the time and opportunity to pursue his real career as a train robber.

'What'll we do with them?' the stranger asked.

The mayor smiled. 'Very simple.' He nodded toward the bedroom door. 'That room has no windows. Put them in there.'

The hatchet-faced man nodded to Bart and

166

Maggie. They went inside, and the door closed on them, leaving them in complete darkness. They heard a key turn in the lock.

Then Mayor Peters spoke loudly enough for them to hear him. 'I hope this will not inconvenience you two. And I assure you both of an excellent burial in any event.'

After that they could hear the two men arguing and moving around for several minutes. Then there was silence. It could only mean the two were on their way to Willow Ridge and the unfortunate old people.

Bart frowned in the darkness. 'I certainly gave them all the information they needed.'

'You couldn't have guessed about the mayor,' Maggie consoled him.

'I should have,' he complained. 'Everything pointed here to Durez City, but I thought young Kingston was Texas Jack.'

'Surely he won't hurt his own father and mother,' she said.

'They're both vicious killers,' Bart warned. 'They can make certain nobody finds out about them if they kill the old people—and us.'

'Surely someone will come,' she said. 'Perhaps you can break open the door, if they've gone.'

He nodded. 'I've given them enough time now.' And without waiting, he threw his weight against the door. But it didn't budge. He hurled himself against it with renewed effort, and it gave only a little.

He turned to her, breathing hard from his efforts. 'They've put a cabinet or something against it.'

'Bart!' Maggie spoke sharply. 'I smell smoke!'

And she was right. At almost the same instant the acrid smell reached his nostrils. And he knew that the mayor had planned things so they'd not be heard from again. He'd set the old house on fire!

'Don't panic!' he warned her. 'Get down on the floor. The air will be better there.' And he hurled himself at the door with a new energy born of the knowledge they would soon suffocate unless they got free.

Now the dark room seemed to be thick with smoke. He coughed and continued to batter the door, which had moved only a fraction of an inch. He could hear the dry crackle of flames, and the air was becoming insufferably hot.

He bent close to Maggie, coughing and struggling for breath as he groped to put an arm around her. 'Make one last try,' he gasped.

As he stumbled toward the door again, he heard new sounds: voices in loud confusion on the other side of the door. And one of them belonged to Doc Webster.

It took only seconds for the rescue party to pull the heavy cabinet from the door and free the almost suffocated Bart and Maggie. It was some minutes after they were safely outside before Bart could think clearly.

Doc Webster was there, along with Sheriff Hill and his deputy. They formed a forlorn little group in the darkness as they stood watching the old house being devoured by flames. Ten minutes later, rescue would have been out of the question, and only their lifeless bodies would have been dragged from the smoke-filled room.

Maggie was stretched out on a blanket the sheriff had placed on the grass. She was still suffering from shock and coughing. Bart's throat felt as if he had actually swallowed some of the flames enveloping the building. The roof caved in as they watched, sending out a great shower of sparks near them.

Bart turned to the sheriff. 'Texas Jack and the Kingstons' son are headed for Willow Ridge. I've got to try to catch up to them before they get there.'

Sheriff Hill, who had been told enough of the facts to understand Bart was a marshal and the mayor was Texas Jack, was not optimistic. 'They'll be there by now,' he said.

'I doubt it,' Bart told him. 'They're using the carriage to pick up the gold. They can't make too much time.' He paused and added grimly, 'If I can get there, I've still got a little surprise for them.'

'Better leave it to the sheriff, Bart,' Doc

169

Webster said with a worried expression on his bloated face. 'You've had your share of luck. If Maggie hadn't come out here and the sheriff and I after her, you'd be dead right now. Better stop while you're ahead.'

'Tonight will finish it,' Bart said, and ran off toward the barn to get the bay.

A few minutes later he was on the trail to Willow Ridge, with the blazing farmhouse only a dull red reflection in the dark sky behind him. The sheriff and his deputy were following, while Doc Webster had remained to look after Maggie.

The trail, or what had once been one, threaded through a cool timber belt of straggly piñon and sleeker junipers. He urged the bay along at a gallop. The country became rockier and more rugged than that which lay behind him. Willow Ridge was a mile straight ahead.

He spurred the bay on. The horse went up the rough incline with its ears pinned back. The trail wound crazily, Bart figured they must have had to travel slowly with the carriage. This would be in his favor. In a few minutes he would know for certain. And he cursed himself for so glibly having revealed everything to Texas Jack and prayed that he might arrive in time to save the two helpless old people.

At last he came in sight of the lodge and paused on the hilltop above it. There were lights shining from its windows, and the

170

carriage was still in front of the door. He could see motion as the two outlaws carted out the several wooden cases of gold. He watched with grim satisfaction. Maybe he could manage it yet!

He headed the bay slowly down toward the scene of activity and over rough ground to get there by the most direct route. The trail was tricky, and impatience gnawed at him as, his .45 ready, he let the bay gingerly pick its way over a shaly downslope.

And then he knew they had spotted him. Even in the darkness, they had known he was near. The sound of the horse's hooves would help them to locate him. Since there was no longer any hope of concealment, he rode boldly toward the carriage. The two outlaws exchanged excited cries and swung up on the seat of the carriage. One of them turned to fire at Bart. There was an orange glow, and a bullet clipped by his head. He pushed the bay on.

Now the carriage was hurtling along the rocky trail, and he was gaining on it with each succeeding moment. They left the lodge in the mad race. Now he was nearing the swaying carriage, was so near he could hear the shouts and curses of the two outlaws. Several times one of them wheeled around to shoot at him, but the swaying vehicle made decent aim impossible, and none of the bullets reached Bart.

Then it was his turn to try some shots. But he didn't attempt to hit either of the outlaws. Instead, he directed the .45 at the wooden cases in the rear of the carriage, which made an easier target. He fired twice without result. And then, as the carriage struck more even ground and the distance between them grew a little wider, he fired a third shot.

This hit the target he was aiming for. There was a great roar and flash of light, followed by a tremendous, swelling cloud of dust. He reined the frightened bay back on its haunches and held his head down until the explosion subsided. And he thanked the foresight that had made him pack one of the gold boxes with dynamite. The outlaws hadn't had time to notice. And unwittingly they had loaded the means of their destruction aboard the carriage with them.

When the dust settled, he got off the bay and went forward on foot to study the wreckage. He was still standing there when Sheriff Hill and his deputy rode up.

'What in thunder happened?' the burly sheriff wanted to know as he dismounted.

Bart jerked his head toward the wreckage of the wagon and the remains of the two horses. 'Texas Jack and Kingston are there somewhere,' he said grimly. 'But only the vultures will be able to find them.'

'What about the gold?'

Bart gave a rueful smile. 'I reckon a good part of it is salted back in the ground. We'd better see how the old people are.'

The three of them rode back together and found the Kingstons bound and gagged on the floor of the lodge. But no other harm had come to them. Whatever plans the two outlaws had had for them, they hadn't had time to carry them through.

The saga of Texas Jack was to become a legend of Durez City. The cow town quickly got a new undertaker, and a reformed or at least slightly less alcoholic Doc Webster became the new mayor. And Sheriff Hill kept his job.

Marshal Bart Landry saw that enough of his reward money went to the Kingstons to build them a nice little cottage in town. He stayed in Durez City only for a few days before he said goodbye to Maggie Malone and went on to another assignment.

Maggie turned out to be a very efficient businesswoman. She hired a manager to run the saloons and cleared the ranch of Nick Cressy and his hoodlums. With the new cowpokes she brought in from Santa Ana, she put the Diamond O on a paying basis.

Eve Driscoll went back East to live and married a stockbroker there. Her father put the Lazy T up for sale and went to live with her. It was about a month after the Lazy T was advertised that Marshal Bart Landry rode into

Durez City on the bay. He didn't even stop to say hello to the new mayor, Doc Webster. Instead, he went straight to the real estate agent's office and then out to the Diamond O.

Maggie Malone came out of the ranch house as he drove up. She'd seen a rider approaching and hadn't been able to believe it was Bart until he came closer. Two years had made her even prettier. The roguish blue eyes were wide with delight as she came up to him.

'You said you'd be back one day,' she told him with a smile.

He got off the bay and took her by the arms. 'When I had finished with marshaling,' he said. 'I'd never marry a girl to make her a marshal's widow.'

'Are you still a marshal?' she asked.

'Gave it up one week ago at six p.m.,' he said with an easy smile. 'And today I bought me the Lazy T spread. How would you like to leave this place and be a rancher's wife?'

'A lot better than being a marshal's widow,' she said softly, her eyes laughing as he took her in his arms for a kiss.

174